TELL TALES

Totally Amazing Little Exciting Stories

From Around The UK Vol II

Edited by Lynsey Hawkins

Disclaimer

Young Writers has maintained every effort
to publish stories that will not cause offence.

Any stories, events or activities relating to individuals
should be read as fictional pieces and not construed
as real-life character portrayal.

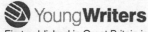 Young**Writers**
First published in Great Britain in 2006 by:
Young Writers
Remus House
Coltsfoot Drive
Peterborough
PE2 9JX
Telephone: 01733 890066
Website: www.youngwriters.co.uk

SB ISBN 1 84602 649 0

Foreword

Young Writers was established in 1991 and has been passionately devoted to the promotion of reading and writing in children and young adults ever since. The quest continues today. *Young Writers* remains as committed to engendering the fostering of burgeoning poetic and literary talent as ever.

This year, *Young Writers* are happy to present a dynamic and entertaining new selection of the best creative writing from a talented and diverse cross-section of some of the most accomplished secondary school writers around. Entrants were presented with four inspirational and challenging themes.

'Myths And Legends' gave pupils the opportunity to adapt long-established tales from mythology (whether Greek, Roman, Arthurian or more conventional eg The Loch Ness monster) to their own style.

'A Day In The Life Of ...' offered pupils the chance to depict twenty-four hours in the lives of literally anyone they could imagine. A hugely imaginative wealth of entries were received encompassing days in the lives of everyone from the top media celebrities to historical figures like Henry VIII or a typical soldier from the First World War.

Finally 'Short Stories', in contrast, offered no limit other than the author's own imagination! 'Ghost Stories' challenged pupils to write an old-fashioned ghost story, relying on suspense, tension and terror rather than using violence and gore.

Telling T.A.L.E.S. From Around The UK Vol II is ultimately a collection we feel sure you will love, featuring as it does the work of the best young authors writing today.

Contents

Michael Padfield (13)   37
James Aucote (13)   38
Chloé Hunwick (12)   39
Daniel Watson (12)   40
Aaron Rawlinson (13)   41
Laura Lindsay (13)   42
Shakila Chowdhury (12)   43
Neil Conway (13)   44
Sarah Waring (13)   45
Lauren Carter (13)   46

Ferrers Specialist Arts College, Rushden
Emma Travill (14)   47
Rebekah Byer (14)   48
Alex Rudgalvis (14)   49
Rebecca Mantle (14)   50
Holly Smith (14)   51
Rachel Wharwood (14)   52
Megan Williams (14)   53
Beth Pearman (13)   54
Laura Kirkup (13)   55
Katie Jackson (14)   56
Robyn Hoddell (13)   57
Kirstie Hawthornthwaite (13)   58
Harry Fletcher (14)   59
Martin Burke (15)   60
Jason Peace (14)   61
Cameron Bower (13)   62
James Neagle (14)   63
Hannah Edwards (13)   64
Aaron Gilson (14)   65
Scott Winfrow (14)   66
Bailey Helsdown (13)   67

Granville Community School, Swadlincote
Nicola Ashington (14)   68
Scott Barnett (14)   69
Natasha Williams (14)   70
Stacey Jewell (13)   71
Kelly Lawrence (14)   72
Natalie Thomas (13)   73

Tyla Houlton (14)	74
Jodie Litchfield (14)	75
Kirsty Griffiths (14)	76
Gemma Bark (13)	77
Phillip King (13)	78
Daniel Ellis (13)	80
Katie Griffiths (13)	81
Natasha Joseph (13)	82
Holly Banton (12)	83
Hannya Brown (13)	84
Laura Fearn (13)	85
Lauren Griffiths (13)	86
Peter Wright (13)	87
Andrew Billings (13)	88
Amy Beaman (12)	89

Humphrey Perkins High School & Community Centre, Loughborough

Lauren Bailey (12)	90
Bethany Kell (13)	91
Lydia Hall (12)	92
Jade Kunne (13)	93
Joanne Paul (13)	94
Jessica Ball (13)	95
James Myers (13)	96
Amy Hunter (12)	97
Abigail Bates (13)	98
Matthew Mills (12)	99

Trinity Catholic High School, Woodford Green

Richard Pniewski (14)	100
Claire Mulvey (15)	101
Alisha Cullen (15)	102
Daniel Meader (15)	103
Lewis Board (15)	104
Charlie Bostock (15)	105
Channing Gardner (12)	106
Charlotte Carnell (12)	107
Vivien Bodnar (12)	108
Kate Underwood (12)	109
Rosie Bostock (12)	110

The Creative Writing

The Man

Have you ever noticed someone standing somewhere day after day and thought, *who is he?* or *why is he standing there?* 90% of the time this person would be totally innocent … Well, this is my story.

A man stood at the end of my street, he had dark fuzzed hair and wore tatted boots every day. As you'd pass him you'd get a whiff of smoke and rotten eggs. He stood there for about a week. The type of person you would normally avoid, but when you had to walk past him you'd keep your eyes fixed and say nothing … well you know what I'm getting at.

One day, as I walked to my friend's house, I had to pass him. He followed at a distance. I thought to myself, *is he stalking me or just heading in the same direction?* So I decided to turn right at the next street, he followed. I shouted to my friend (who really wasn't there) 'Dan Dan, wait.' I ran down the street, as fast as I could, fear driving me.

Anyway, I hid in a small bush between two sheds. I shuffled to the back, kept perfectly still and held my breath until he passed … and that was the last I saw of him.

I wondered about him for days and finally convinced myself that he could just have been going to his friend's house. But then I heard on the news weeks later that a man was imprisoned for murder, a man with fuzzed hair, tatted boots, who stalked his victims before murdering them!

Just think, that could have been me!

Tommy Rutter (13)
Biddick School & Sports College, Washington

Like She's Never Before!

'Emma have you seen my pink bikini top?' I shouted. I yanked open my bottom drawer and emptied the entire contents onto the floor.

'No I haven't, I'm kinda busy myself you know!' Emma yelled back, her voice was muffled. She was obviously in the back of her wardrobe, doing the same thing, last minute packing, we were never organised it was like a family tradition, huh we were going to a big dance competition. Soon enough we were packed and ready to go, we both raced downstairs when we heard the car furiously beeping.

We finally arrived, I tucked my fringe behind my ears and adjusted my bikini top, we were first on stage. 'Good luck Jenna,' Emma whispered.

I stepped forward and took the mic; 'She's a maniac, a maniac on the floor, she's dancing like she's never danced before.' I stood back and watched Emma do the first moves then it came to me, I ran forward and did three backflips, two walk-overs and finished by going back into a bridge. Emma flipped over me and we both got up and danced out moves, fast vicious, smooth and cool. The audience was going crazy for us, the cameras were flashing and the cheering got louder. The dance was over, we went to get our photos for the dance mag.

Hours passed, it came to the final moment, 'And the winners ...'

Becky Mitchell (12)
Biddick School & Sports College, Washington

Am I Cursed?

I came out of work. Got into my Audi and drove home. On the way home, I was struck at the front of my car by another car. I could just make out the shadow lying over the steering wheel of the car. I ended up in hospital with a few broken bones. A couple of hours later I still couldn't move a muscle, so I had to take it easy.

But when I came home from the hospital my house had been trashed so badly, I thought I was hallucinating but I wasn't. I tried to my phone but as I reached it the wire had been cut so I reached into my bag and pulled out my mobile phone. I rang the police, they said they'd come as soon as possible.

By the time they arrived I was so worked up about it and I had to go and live with my mam for a few weeks while my dad sorted out my house. A few days later the police came and said they couldn't find the culprit so I suggested the man who'd driven into me, but they said he had been killed in the trauma.

Eventually I came home and it took me a while to get settled in.

Three years later - I became pregnant and had a little girl called Natalia. As she grew up she became very close to me and had a very good job.

One day on the way home from work she got struck by another car, and she had the same injuries as me, so the hospital rang me and told me to come right away. So when we came out of the hospital and went to her house. As we went in everything had been trashed, the phone wire had been cut, but we heard a noise. So I went to check it out. I froze …

Jade Clements (12)
Biddick School & Sports College, Washington

A Trip To The Hospital

'Pass, pass!' I shouted as my brother, Adam, ran past me with the ball. I started to run so I could take a shot. He never passed but he did shoot, bam, the ball curled into the back of the net. Adam and I celebrated as the keeper went to get the ball from the other side of the hill. When he got back he kicked off and I slipped and fell onto something sharp and split my knee open, but I didn't know until I lifted up my trouser leg and shouted to Adam.

He started to laugh and came over and suddenly stopped and looked. At this point the blood had turned my white sock red. Adam and Josh rushed me home and Josh was muttering to himself, 'I didn't see his leg.' Josh started to run and got my mam.

When I got home my mam and dad decided to take me to the hospital. I waited to see the nurse and she cleaned my leg very gently, but couldn't get a piece of my trouser leg out.

Five minutes later she was finished and she told us to wait so I could see the doctor and she would tell me if I would need stitches or not.

My mam and I waited for three hours watching everyone going to see her, until it came to my turn. I hobbled to my bed and got told I needed two to three stitches and I went to the room where I had an X-ray.

Then went to get my stitches and had four put in my leg. I went home with some tablets to help the cut heal and not get infected.

I left the hospital at 10 o'clock and arrived home at 10.25 and was told to keep my leg elevated for 24 hours, and had to miss school. I went to sleep in five seconds flat, I was so tired.

I woke up the next morning thinking it was all a dream, but it wasn't. I felt the patch on my leg and realised it was real. I made my way downstairs and lay on the sofa, and watched TV until I wrote this story for my homework!

Jonathan Foster (12)
Biddick School & Sports College, Washington

The Storm

It was summer 1954. It was forecast for just light showers but the weather ladies were hardly ever right.

It all started when the sky was turning a pale yellow, as the storm grew louder. It was two in the morning; I was sitting in my bedroom alone. I was scared, the trees made shadows all around my room like great big hands grasping me, making me shiver. All of a sudden there was a strike of lightning, this made me more frightened. I was shaking like a wet dog on a cold day,but still I remember I heard it, it still scares me after four years. The voices all around me travelling in the gale.

As time grew I began to get more scared, I began to shout, no sound could be heard except the loud screech from the wild whirling tornado that was heading straight my way. I put my head under the bedcovers, nothing was helping, it grew louder and louder. My bed started to shake, I tried to shout, it was no good. Suddenly it stopped... Then I woke up. I still don't know still to this day whether it was a dream or not.

Christina Savage (12)
Biddick School & Sports College, Washington

KD

It's hard being a KD because you have to get told off by your teachers because you cannot do your homework. I cannot do the other things a boy my age should do. In case you're wondering a KD is Kid Detective, and I am an expert.

I was walking home from another detention today when I saw William Walker getting pushed around by some boys from school.

'Oi man! Leave William alone!' I shouted across the road. William was in the same class as me in school and he was always getting picked on simply because of his intelligence. He was extremely bright. I marched across the road to see it was Brad Armstrong who was picking on him. Brad was the local bully with bright, curly ginger hair and freckles. He had behavioural problems and his mam and dad were always getting into trouble with the police.

'What are you going to do about it? You think you're solid just because you don't do your homework?' he snapped back rudely. William saw the opportunity to run away because Brad wasn't paying attention anymore on him. He was more interested in having an argument with me. I walked away despite getting showered with abuse. I was trained to do that.

The next day at school William wasn't there. I didn't think much about it until a few days later when he still hadn't come in for school. I decided to call at his house because he never missed school. His dad answered the door looking very distraught.

'He's gone missing! I'm sure he has! He hasn't left a note or anything and he's sent no emails to anyone. I've contacted all of his friends and they haven't seen him,' he explained.

'Calm down, Mr Walker. I'm sure we'll find him safe and sound,' I assured him. I sincerely hope that I am right. After retracing all of the links, there was one question that was bamboozling me: Had he run away or had he been kidnapped? ...

Matthew Hall (11)
Biddick School & Sports College, Washington

The Party

'Mum I'm going over to Jake's house, we need to do some homework,' lied Sarah. She wanted to go to a party that she knew she never would be allowed to go to.

'OK, but I don't want you home late,' said her mum.

She had got away with it.

She left the house and headed for the nearest bush. She got her party outfit on then left her other clothes in the bush and headed to the party. As she arrived at the party, she was surprised to see that everyone was older than her. She started walking around. She saw tins and bottles, and a group of boys who she thought were doing drugs. She met up with her friend who was allowed at the party. She was old enough to drive, so she decided to drive them home. As they got into the car a group of boys followed them. They were driving all over the place and following Sarah and her friend. The boys started speeding up and were driving uncontrollably.

The next day Sarah's mum got a phone call from the Emergency Room. 'Hello Mrs Bradley, I'm sorry your daughter was in an accident last night ...'

Her mum never had a chance to say goodbye.

Shelby Hall (13)
Biddick School & Sports College, Washington

The Haunted House

There was an old house that stood on its own right by a wood and no one would go near because of fear. Nothing went near not even a mouse ...

As you go in there is silence, then all of a sudden *bang!* the door slams closed behind you. You turn round to try and open the door but it is locked. So you try to find another way out, when suddenly you hear someone calling your name and a banging then crying, even though the house has been abandoned for three years. You start walking towards the stairs, you want to stop, but it's as if your mind's being controlled by something else, getting dragged towards the sounds.

In that room there is nothing, wait ... your eyes get dragged to a picture of a mother and a baby. Then a dagger that is on the wall moves, it moves to the picture, then it stabs the picture right in the forehead, then blood drips off onto the picture.

You're scared, spooked and puzzled, then you hear a crying from the next room. You walk in, there's a cot and a mysteriously misty figure standing right next to it, you look next to you and there's a baby lying next to you, but it wasn't there before. Then you turn back to the figure and it fades away, then you hear the doors creaking open and you run for safety, taking the baby with you.

Lyndsey Brown (13)
Biddick School & Sports College, Washington

Bullying

Beth and I were in her bedroom. I thought if I could talk to her face to face I could find out why she had been upset for the past week. While she went to the toilet I picked up her pillow to put on the floor and as I did a little pink book fell on the floor. It said on the cover 'Beth's Diary', but I thought if I read her diary then I might find out why she was upset. I looked around and made sure she wasn't looking, and I picked it up. I opened the first page and it said:

'Monday 4th October.

Dear Diary, Kathryn was calling me and she threatened to hit me again. I really don't know what to do because it's been happening for over two months now. I want to tell Lucy but I don't know if I can in case she says something to Kathryn'.

'Tuesday 5th October.

Dear Diary, today was even worse I think Kathryn was trying to make friends with Lucy today, but Lucy didn't go with her. She put a pin my chair and I sat on it. It really hurt and Kathryn was laughing at me. I don't want to go to school tomorrow I'm too scared'.

I looked up and turned over the page.

'Wednesday 6th October.

Dear Diary, I was off today I said to my mam and dad I was ill so I didn't have to see Kathryn'.

I turned over the page again.

'Thursday 7th October.

Dear Diary, I was at school again today. Kathryn tripped me over and I have hurt all my leg'.

I took a deep breath and turned over the page.

'Friday 8th October.

Dear Diary, it's the last day today! Lucy is sleeping over tomorrow I'm going to tell her about everything because I need to tell someone and I know I can tell her'.

I looked and heard her coming. As she opened the door there I stood holding her diary. I thought to myself, *will she tell me?*

I smiled and told her everything would be okay, and I think it's not the best thing to read people's diaries, but it did help in this tricky situation.

Danielle Wilson (13)
Biddick School & Sports College, Washington

Haunted House

'Who wants to go on holiday?' shouted William. William was married and had two kids, Alan and Jamie. Alan and Jamie were ten-year-old twins and their mom, Stacy, was a travel agent. Every now and again she got free holidays. The family had decided to go to Florida and they were all very excited.

As the time grew nearer they started shopping for clothes. Soon the holiday was here.

'Let's go everyone,' said Stacy.

When they were all in the car, William put the radio on. it was talking about Florida.

'Everybody listen, it's where we're going,' said William.

'There have been a few reports about a castle being haunted, so stay out of there,' said the reporter.

'Cool. A haunted castle! We have to go,' said Alan.

'No, didn't you hear him? He said we should stay out,' replied Jamie.

'I'm sure it's not really haunted,' said Stacy.

When they got there, straight away they saw the castle.

'Let's go and look around,' said Stacy.

When they got to the castle, it was completely deserted.

'Hey this is great! There'll be no more queues!' said Alan.

'But maybe it's because it's haunted!' replied Jamie.

'Wimp!' said Alan.

They looked around at all the statues and sculptures.

'I'm bored now. Can we go?' asked Alan.

'No, you wanted to come, so we'll stay for a bit,' replied Stacy.

Suddenly they heard such a clatter that they all jumped.

'See! This place *is* haunted!' screamed Jamie.

'Mommy, help me!' cried Alan, turning to Stacy.

But she was gone …

Helen Campbell (13)
Biddick School & Sports College, Washington

The Fairy At The End Of The Garden

It was the beginning of the summer holidays! I pushed my cover away, swinging my legs round, allowing my feet to find my pink fluffy slippers. I decided to have my breakfast out onto the patio, it was such a lovely day.

I put my toast and juice on the table outside. I was about to sit down when suddenly I heard a splash in the pond. I walked over slowly wondering what it could have been. To my amazement, there sitting on a lily pad was a fairy.

'Hello,' I whispered.

She looked up slowly. 'Hi,' she replied, nervously.

'Can I help you little fairy?' I asked.

'I'm not sure, I keep trying to fly but it doesn't seem to be working,' she said pitifully.

I held out my hand and she hopped on, then I carefully carried her upstairs and placed her in my dolls' house. She bounced on the bed happily talking non-stop, her shyness disappearing quickly. She made her way up the little stairs to the balcony at the top of the house. The only problem was I had not seen my cat Molly come in, she'd seen my little fairy and wanted to play. The fairy saw Molly and got such a shock, she slipped and seemed to fall in slow motion for ages. Suddenly she started flapping her little wings, she swept through the air, and then landed safely on my chest of drawers. 'I flew, I flew!' she shouted jumping up and down in the air. I was so happy she had learned how to fly.

We stayed friends, and she is now living in the dolls' house at the end of the garden.

Lauren Bell (12)
Biddick School & Sports College, Washington

The Dark Woods

It was a dark and stormy night. The residents of Little Haggleton were afraid. They feared the lashing wind, the crunching waves and above all the darkening shadow.

Every night of the full moon, anyone wandering in the dark woods disappeared mysteriously.

In the wood there was an ancient evil, the dark shadow would pass over them, screaming, then a hideous howl, the next day only bones would be left.

One night a guy called Jack had been drinking. He cared little of the monster but just to be sure he carried a revolver.

'You are not going into the woods are you?' his mates asked hurriedly.

'You don't believe in such things do you?' Jack sniggered. 'So who is going to come with me? No one, fine, I will go myself,' and with that Jack disappeared in the gloom.

It quickly became dark in the woods. Jack got nervous and had the distinct feeling of being watched. As he passed an ancient oak he ran, the hideous yelping behind him, then remembering his gun he turned and shot.

The creature shrugged off the hit and came into the light. It was a werewolf. In seconds it was onto him and everyone knew what happened next …

Jack's funeral was held the following week.

Andrew Lunn (13)
Biddick School & Sports College, Washington

Duel

The man pulled out a long silver sword. It glinted in the afternoon sunlight. A heavy thud echoed across the mountain top as the sword struck black armour. A cold wind whipped into the two knights' eyes.

'Think you can beat me, Arthur?' the knight in black laughed. The knight pulled out a black sword, gripping it tightly in two hands. He swung, striking Arthur's sword. Arthur stumbled a few steps backwards.

'Yes, actually I do.' Arthur charged forward, swinging his sword with great power. The black knight blocked, twirling his sword as Arthur took a few more steps backwards. He sighed. 'So young.' The knight lunged forward, his attacks striking off Arthur's sword. Arthur stared back at Blake. 'I'm more talented than you'll ever be,' replied Arthur. He twirled his sword in his hand. Blake tossed his hair back and laughed so loud the nearby birds darted from their hiding places. Arthur spun around, attacking Blake with speed and power. The black knight blocked, his face twisted into an expression of hate. The blades struck off each other countless times, each attack as ineffective as the last.

'You know,' said Blake, 'you're not that bad. Ever thought of joining us? You'd do well.'

'I'll never join that corrupt gang of thugs.'

Blake snarled, throwing all his anger into the strikes. Arthur's face showed his concentration. The two swords locked in a cross shape. Arthur quickly rolled, releasing Excalibur from the lock. Blake's sword fell to the ground. Arthur pointed his sword towards the sky. He thrust it upwards, cutting a perfect hole in Blake's throat. Blake's eyes widened. His hands grabbed his throat. Blake's lifeless body crumpled to the floor.

Adam Dawson (13)
Biddick School & Sports College, Washington

The Sleepover

I sat at my desk, staring through the old faded glass of the classroom and out into the winter gloom of Seaview Road. The whole class seemed to be drowning in boredom and I guessed that they would be watching the clock anxiously for 3pm to approach.

At last the loud ringing of the school bell could be heard from the dark corridor outside. I jumped to my feet, collected my coat and left. I couldn't wait to get home. It was Friday and I was going to my friend's house along with three others from our class. We were having a sleepover, but not just any sleepover, a sleepover in the most haunted house in our town. Blackberry Mansion.

At 9pm all five of us sat by a warm, crackling fire. Having eaten many bars of chocolate we were all ready to tell ghost stories. It would have been fun that's if Keisha (the eldest of us) hadn't have found that ouija board. It might have all ended differently.

We all sat around the old board and glass in silence.

'Well!' Keisha began. 'Who's in?'

Nobody answered.

'Scared!' she repeated over and over again until we all gave up and the game began.

'Is there anybody there?' Keisa mocked.

Nothing happened. She repeated her sentence. Suddenly the glass shot across the board. The lights went out and flashed back on. Keisha was gone, gone never to be seen again.

Claire Savage (13)
Biddick School & Sports College, Washington

Howay The Lads

I walked out of the changing rooms looking straight at the pitch and not the player standing next to me. My heart pounded like a beating drum as I heard the crowd of 52,500 magnificent Geordie fans roaring for their football club, Newcastle United, which was like a god to them, and me, Matthew Weightman, the golden number 9 on the back of my shirt gleamed in the sun. I jogged onto the holy football pitch almost deafened by the roars as the Newcastle team sheet was read out and heard around the glorious stands.

The referee's whistle blew and echoed throughout my body and the world seemed to stop for a second or two, before I knew it I had the ball at my feet, I danced round one or two Man United players. The crowd egged me to go on but I didn't. I stopped, laid the ball back neatly to one of my players.

As every second and every minute passed so quickly, my body became more tired and more dirty as the opposing players kicked me to the ground. I looked to the ref and then my manager, but he just looked back with his arms folded and walked back to the dugout just as the half-time whistle blew. 0-0. For the first time we were booed and rightly so we were awful. The second half began, as it ended, the crowd were unsettled and that isn't good. Ninety minutes gone, still we were tied. I had the ball at my feet. I went round 1, 2, 3, then the goalie, *goal!* I celebrated with the fans in delight and then …

'Wake up, wake up, you'll be late for school!'

Matthew Weightman (13)
Biddick School & Sports College, Washington

New Beginnings

The doorbell rang for the fourth time that week. Another letter to be signed for, another summons for court. I couldn't believe I had allowed myself to get into this mess!

The journey to work was endless my mind was so distracted. What was I to do? It was my turn to do the banking that day. Such a lot of money - *oh the troubles would be gone if it were mine,* was the thought in my head.

I headed towards the tube station with a briefcase, inside safely locked away was that week's takings. I could feel the warm sun on my face as I dodged my way through the city crowds. Oh blow it! I couldn't be bothered to sink into the darkness of the tube.

I thought I would catch the Number 17 bus instead to stay in the sunshine; after all I may be locked away in a dark cell this time next week, after the court appearance.

What was that noise! Such a commotion ahead. Sirens, police, utter chaos. A police officer informed me of a massive fire in the tube - *disaster.* Or was it? Could it have been my saving grace - a moral dilemma! Should I have continued my journey, or fled with the cash!

I like to consider that I have been a good person, but it hasn't done me much good. People take advantage you see.

Without further thought I swiftly changed direction and hailed a black cab. 'Heathrow airport, please.'

And now I'm sitting outside a little Greek taverna sipping a cold beer. My new life - new beginnings.

Amy Bennett (12)
Fair Oak Business & Enterprise College, Rugeley

Living The Life Of A Bee

Hello, I'm Bob the bee. I have 80 brothers and sisters and they are called Bill, Ben, Mini Bob etc … My mum and dad are called Betty and Benny. Today I'm going to tell you a story, 'The best day of my life'.

28th July 2005, the best day of my life.

I was buzzing around the berry bush when I saw Lady, a dog from the house. She came trotting up to me and barked madly at me. I quickly flew off. Unfortunately, she chased me into the house. I panicked as a tall human approached me with a magazine …

The man lifted it up and brought it down … Then a big, blurry object stood in front of me. 'Don't hit him, he's cute,' yelled the object. It was then I found out, that it was a girl called Ellie. She picked me up and carried me to safety.

She placed me in a box. 'Hello you're safe now,' whispered Ellie. The box had a bed, tables, everything I'd ever dreamed of, a home. I stayed there for about a week, then Ellie placed me in a huge box with 83 beds! I then realised she wanted me and my whole family to move in. So I flew out and got my whole family and we moved in!

We now live in a home with Ellie and she looks after us. We fly about every day then fly back home. My home.

Katie Holloway (12)
Fair Oak Business & Enterprise College, Rugeley

The Scariest Day

Every second I was kneeling there my heart was pounding in my chest, as if a thousand horses were trapped and were trying to break free, but failing. I heard their footsteps coming nearer, a million thoughts going through my head making me throb with pain and all the pain stopped at three simple words.

'Kill the girl.'

At that moment I jumped up screaming and made a dash for the door. Oh it was locked, so I ran for the window. I could feel their breath on the back of my neck.

I was cornered. They were closing in on me, their cold, fierce eyes burning a hole through my stomach. Their cloaks as black as the night covering their faces. Who were they? Did they have family? I didn't know.

He pulled out a large, sharp knife. 'Now it is time to meet your doom,' he boomed. My stomach felt like it would fall through my butt, and there was a large lump in my throat like when you dry-swallow a large pill. Wait a minute, I felt a little draught on the back of my head - a window! I tried hard to wedge it open but it was stuck. So I grabbed the nearest thing and threw it at the window. I jumped out. Running, I was running for my life literally. I could feel them close behind me. I could see a police car. 'Help!' I screeched. They fled as the police car stopped.

Later on, at the station, I told the police what had happened. That was the scariest day of my life.

Lauren Carthy (12)
Fair Oak Business & Enterprise College, Rugeley

The Invasion Of The Xyfral

Deep in the vast universe, far away, in a distant galaxy lived the deadly, mysterious Xyfral race. They are extremely strong, agile and intelligent. They are endlessly amazing creatures with their giant claws, slim and muscular bodies. They are the ultimate predators.

Earth somehow discovered Xyfral's secret existence and now Xyfral think Earth know too much.

The Xyfral leader calls an immediate invasion to purge the human race completely.

So they strike at midnight and they formulate a plan. They assassinate people and spread mysterious rays all over the world that kill people in their sleep. When morning comes, the Xyfral battleships shoot back to space keeping watch from above.

Later that day, millions of people are reported dead and the world now thinks judgement day has arrived.

All but a group of experienced astronauts are afraid of this terrorisation.

So the astronauts gear up, ready to fight this menace. They shoot into space, afraid of the true terror that awaits.

They finally come to mysterious ships and they land on one, just about dodging the plasma pulses shooting at their ship.

They break into the ship and the Xyfral await them. They shoot their guns frantically. *Bang. Bang.*

They finally realise there are too many so they retreat, just about getting away. They plant a bomb and flee. They crash-land back on Earth. An almighty explosion is seen in the sky. The astronauts wonder, *have we seen the last of them ... ?*

Darius Franklin (13)
Fair Oak Business & Enterprise College, Rugeley

Moto

It was the morning of all mornings, I got up and had a wash. Today I had to race Stefan Everts, Paul Edmunson and Dale Winton for the World Championship. I had breakfast and then got in the truck and drove to Branston. He unloaded the bike out of the truck and our mechanics checked the bike over.

I lined up and started my bike. I was nervous. I got ready, the man dropped the gates. I was off. I was third when we went round the corner, but over the table top and round the inner bend I was second. Then on the last lap I went over a jump and whipped it large, and overtook Stefan Everts, and then won. My family was ecstatic. I am world champion.

Ryan Starkey (12)
Fair Oak Business & Enterprise College, Rugeley

The Truth Below ...

Joe's spacecraft lay still in the near distance, burning, totally destroyed. He had to get away from it before it exploded or something. He had probably made it about half a kilometre from the craft before he saw the crater, a huge crater, with purple vein-like tubes twisting into the centre. He had no choice but to follow where they went. The explosion had killed his shipmates. He had lost total communication with Earth due to some weird interference. Though there was little gravity, one step into the dark void left Joe tumbling slowly through the deep shaft, falling past the pulsing tubes, past rocks and then, past nothing.

Joe suddenly reached out desperately ... nothing ... the tubes and rocks had disappeared and had been replaced with a huge empty pit. *Slam!* Joe's body hit the floor with a tremendous force. After minutes on the floor, Joe managed to heave himself up. Something was wrong. There should not have been this much gravity on the moon. He saw that a few metres above him, the purple tubes had mingled to form one twisted length of pipe. The radio in Joe's helmet suddenly sparked to life: 'Hello, hello is anyone there? This is Ground Control. Please copy...'

'This is Joe Barnes, how are you reaching me? My ship is blown up!'

'You must be down the shaft. In that case, goodbye Joe, may God help you.'

'Wait, listen,' said Joe, but the line was dead. Ahead, Joe saw something, a missing robot, it turned, and Joe saw the gleam of two gatling guns ...

Flyn Barrett (13)
Fair Oak Business & Enterprise College, Rugeley

Where The Wild Roses Grow

A long time ago, where the wild roses grow, there was a beautiful young woman named Elisa Day. She lived in the countryside, just a few miles from the village 'Rosenville'.

Her little cottage could barely be seen, through all the roses that clung to the thatched roof. Her window shutters banging in the warm, summer breeze.

Inside there she was, reading a book in her flower-patterned armchair. She sat there so comfy and cosy as the sun shone through, onto the table next to her.

The silence was broken when a loud knock at the door occurred.

As she got up, there was another knock. When she reached the door, she pulled the handle and her heart was beating at a race unknown. She just stood there breathless, for there was the most handsome man standing there. She started to cry. He wiped the tears from her face.

He pulled one arm from behind his back and gave her a rose which matched the bright red colour of her lips, then whispered in her ear and strolled off, leaving her standing in the doorway.

The next day, he came again, and they shared their first kiss. Then came for the next following days.

Therefore he came the next day and asked her to follow him to the river, 'Where the wild roses grow'!

He gave her another rose, then picked up a rock and shouted, 'All beauty must die,' and planted a rose between her teeth, then whispered, 'you are the wild rose!'

Shannon-Louise Hart (13)
Fair Oak Business & Enterprise College, Rugeley

Hide-And-Go-Seek

'Night, see you in the morning Mum,' called Nathan as he trotted up the stairs. He walked onto the springy feather blue carpet of his light blue room. His room was cluttered with his CD collection and clothes he had worn the week before.

As he pounced into his bed, he looked through the window beside him and it was raining. A minute had passed after he had made himself comfortable in his bed, he had fallen fast asleep.

'Come out, come out wherever you are!' snarled a green figure. Running, Nathan slipped, falling into some boxes. The green figure crept closer and closer. With sweat pouring down his aching head he pushed himself even more and ran as fast as he could run.

The green figure started shouting at Nathan, 'You ignorant little child, if you wanted to play hide-and-go-seek why didn't you say?' as he trotted around glancing at Nathan's every visible move.

Nathan ran and ran with all his spirit. He started to feel curious, why was he being chased? Who or what was chasing him? In a daring choice he decided to look behind him, he did and he saw a green figure, that was it, nothing else. Then *bang* he had hit the wall, head-first.

He finally woke up and saw a fat, fuzzy, green figure, in front of him.

'Ahh, brilliant you've woken up, now I can tickle you because I am the tickle monster!' the tickle monster cried.

Liam Fuller (13)
Fair Oak Business & Enterprise College, Rugeley

It

This is the story, a true story of when I met the thing. I called it 'It' back then.

It all happened when I was walking home from school one day. It was cold and the wind was blowing hard. I was wet through, so I decided to take a short cut through a deserted alley. I wouldn't really walk down there normally, but I was really wet.

I slowly tiptoed down the alley when I heard a noise. *Bang!* Then another one. I started running until a figure appeared. It wasn't big but it was taller than me. It started mumbling, so I grabbed a metal pole and threw it at it. I ran as fast as I could until I got home. I quickly ran in and locked the door.

Until this day I've never told anyone about what happened. I've never been down the alley again.

Charlotte Cornfield (12)
Fair Oak Business & Enterprise College, Rugeley

Two Brothers

(This story is based on actual events but happened with larger felines in Africa)

There were two happy cats in Eastern Estonia, one called Buster and one called Suggs. One day they were in the Philippi's backyard having their daily feed of snouts and entrails. Suddenly Buster jolted away as he saw his feline brother being tied up and put in the back of the masked men's rucksack, only with enough air to breathe.

Buster ran after them hoping he could keep the scent of the catnapper. Suggs was a mild-tempered cat with a white, cream-orange and black coat; this was not hard to miss after the gang wars had darkened culture.

Buster ran and ran until his feet were numb because he loved his brother. Suggs was in the back of the van on some cheap mattresses, he roamed around until he found an opening, he gnawed his way through. He jumped out and made his way back the way he had come.

Finally the two brothers found each other in Norly Woods. Suggs explained to Buster what had happened through actions, like falling over, pretending to be unconscious and begging like there was food dangling too high for him to reach.

Sam Dean (12)
Fair Oak Business & Enterprise College, Rugeley

A Tragic Accident

She glided along, semi-transparent, empty white eyes staring into space. Her long white hair hung limp, wisps of dark brown left at the ends. Her nightdress the same shade as her pale face, her feet dangling an inch above the ground. Her terrified screams could still be heard throughout the hospital ever since it had happened, exactly a year ago ...

The story begins when a class of student nurses began a course at the hospital. Opal was particularly smart, always correcting her classmates and finishing set work first. She also argued with them, constantly.

One day when she had been particularly argumentative, some students got together to plan a prank against her. Little did they know the fatal damage they would cause.

The next morning, a male student snuck into Opal's room while she was sleeping and slipped it into her bed. He left and knocked her door, hearing her stir, then a blood-curdling scream. They left, chortling, for their first lesson.

By the end of the day, no one had seen Opal. The matron worriedly knocked on her door, and entered. What she saw caused her to collapse with fright.

The girl was sitting on her bed, face starkly white, her hair now the colour of snow. She was sitting on the ledge of the wide-open window, clutching the amputated arm the student had slipped into her bed. What was most disturbing was that she was gnawing on it.

No one but the police knew what happened to Opal after that ...

Lorna Cowley (13)
Fair Oak Business & Enterprise College, Rugeley

Number 1 ...

It was a normal spring evening in Crackingtonhaven, there was a slight breeze in the air. Abbie's long brown silky hair was blowing in the wind as she was finishing her shift at the local café. She was an intelligent girl who was just starting university. As she was walking around the corner on the way home, a man dressed in a black suit, who she had never seen before, crept behind her like a lion hunting its prey, and covered her mouth with his big hands.

He dragged her along the beach, which was a struggle. Abbie was kicking and trying to scream. He eventually got her to the far end of the beach where nobody could see. He drew a sharp knife out from his pocket and mouthed to her to be quiet, his hand slowly moved away from her mouth, but kept a firm hold on the other arm. She stared at him worryingly and said, 'What do you want?'

'I want you to die ...' he replied calmly not really caring!

She looked at him blankly, there was a long pause, before she could ask why, she was there, lying on the floor, *dead* ... He laid one single red rose on her stab wound and walked off. He chuckled and said to himself, 'Don't worry Abbie there will be more ...'

Alex Darby (13)
Fair Oak Business & Enterprise College, Rugeley

One True Love

To my one and only love, if you are reading this, then I feel for you. As I'm afraid it's for the worst. I'm scared. Scared of losing you. Scared of you forgetting about me. Fighting in the war is at the back of my mind right now; every day I try not to think about what could happen on the front line. It's never quiet. Ever. No time to think and people are constantly being killed. Seeing them is terrible. Many of them were my friends. Watching them die is heart-wrenching, it makes me feel distraught, then I think of their family and the letters they'll no longer be getting. This is no game.

Time goes so slowly here. Another few soldiers got killed today; I couldn't bear to hear the ear-shattering screams and heart-dropping groans for help. You feel so guilty when you leave men there - but there was nothing that I could do, parts of their bodies were scattered across the trench, and there was blood everywhere, which just attracted more rats and fleas. I'd be surprised if they were there tomorrow with those rodents everywhere.

But enough of that talk.

The other day I took my socks off for the first time in ages - and they started moving across the floor!

But remember if I never come back - I'll always be with you.

Always.

All my love Clarence.

World War I ended in November - just one month after this letter was written.

Steph Bennett (13)
Fair Oak Business & Enterprise College, Rugeley

A Boy's Nation

July 30th 1966. One of the proudest moments in English history. The day England won the football World Cup. Ever since that day England has tried to emulate the feat accomplished in 1966. Now in 2006 England feel they have the best chance of winning again, this is the story of 2006.

On 12th May 2006 the England manager announced his squad for the 2006 World Cup with one shock. 18-year-old striker James Hettrick was in that line up. This was way beyond his wildest dreams.

In the first game of the World Cup Hettrick was left on the bench and this continued as England won all three group games and made a date with Italy in the next round. England cruised past the next two rounds but still Hettrick hadn't even come on as a sub.

The semi-finals beckoned for England and world champs Brazil was the team England were against. England started well but Brazil took the lead with a Ronaldinho strike on 42 minutes. England however showed their passion and scored two goals in the last ten minutes. Hettrick didn't even make the bench.

The final, England v Germany. Hettrick started for the first time. Germany scored three goals in an amazing first half, but the second half would be totally different! Hettrick put all pressure behind him and scored four amazing second half goals. He had scored England their first World Cup for forty years.

England owed it all to a teenage boy.

James Hettrick (13)
Fair Oak Business & Enterprise College, Rugeley

The Ocean Pearl

The engines are roaring, my heart is pounding and my feet are shaking. I know this all sounds so dramatic but I'm only sitting on a plane for the first time. I'm on my way to Cairns, Australia, which is right next to the Great Barrier Reef. Wow, imagine all the great stuff I can do, like scuba-diving, building sandcastles, playing on the beach, oh I can't wait.

The seatbelt sign has flashed on now, we're landing. My stomach feels like it's turned upside down. *Bang!* We're on the ground in Australia. My new life is beginning. I'm walking down the steps now into the Australian airport. Looking around I thought there would be kangaroos jumping everywhere, little koalas climbing up trees and men with funny hats saying 'g'day mate', but to my disappointment it was just the same as England.

My mum drove us to our new house; it was a lovely little wooden shack on the edge of the beach. It's perfect, well it's more than I'd ever dreamt. I wanted to explore but as I stepped out the front door, I tumbled over a little wooden box. I was curious, like all people would be, when I flicked up the lock of the box. And then I saw it! A small, white, dainty, little pearl lying there, on a ruby-red pillow. Suddenly I heard a voice and it said, 'Don't mess with the ocean pearl.'

What? I don't understand!

Abi Jones (13)
Fair Oak Business & Enterprise College, Rugeley

A Strange New Land

'Right! That's it! I've had enough!' Sam screamed at her mum. She stormed out, slamming the door behind her. She wandered around in the ever-deepening dusk, the air around her getting colder with each step she took. A shiver ran down her spine. She began to think it wasn't such a good idea, walking out of her house. What if she wasn't allowed back in? She had no friends here; she hated being the 'new girl'. All her family were back in Australia. She had nowhere to go.

Why? Why did we have to move to this rainy, boring, good-for-nothing island? Why did Dad have to get that stupid job promotion? I hate him. I hate all of them. And most of all I hate England.

Sam continued to walk aimlessly to and fro. She had no idea where she was. She hadn't got used to her new neighbourhood and she didn't plan to. She kept hearing strange noises. Each time she comforted herself with, 'it's just the weird animals of this stupid, little country' or 'chill! You know it's just your warped imagination!' but she was finding it hard to convince herself. She let out a little yelp at every noise and finally gave up. She screamed with anguish and fell sobbing against a tree. It hid her with its thick tentacle-like branches… or so she thought.

As she dreamt about her beautiful homeland, the darkness closed in around her …

Emily Adams (13)
Fair Oak Business & Enterprise College, Rugeley

Innocent Yet Guilty

'Run!' she yelled. 'Run!'

I ran as fast as I could without looking back. I knew why I was running and I was scared for Sam as she was the one in the real danger. My head was all in a blur as a mixture of thoughts ran through my mind. The pain in my side grew even more intense as I stopped to check for security guards. One was heading straight towards me but I knew I couldn't run anymore. Sam was long gone by the time my head cleared and I knew what was happening. A security guard with a stern look placed a vice-like grip on my immensely painful right shoulder.

'You're coming down town,' he fumed.

I obeyed immediately, not wanting to get on the wrong side of the law. As I was thrust into a police car a weeping woman came up to me and gave me a long-lasting hug that showed people that this woman, who was a bit of a fuzzy image, cared about me.

I thought the trip to the police station took forever. There was a policeman on either side of me. One of them was handcuffed to me. I felt like a mother who had just lost her child. I couldn't stop crying.

When we got there I was thrust into a jail cell and forced to wear overalls. Here I was, a 20-year-old woman in jail for something she hadn't done.

Suddenly …

Bethany Cottrell (13)
Fair Oak Business & Enterprise College, Rugeley

A Knight's Dream!

One day, Wattie and Tunny were walking through the town of Isafer, the home of the elves. With traps littered all around the place, it was no place for the faint-hearted. Wattie and Tunny were there to do business, in order to get a legendary weapon. An aggressive arrowless bow, the amazing elf bow, it shone sparkling silver. They walked dodging the traps, they knew this place back to front. Eventually they found them. Two short elves, dressed in green shirts and shorts. In their hands held bows.

Wattie started towards the one elf, 'In order to get the bow you must defeat the great legendary Calfite Queen!' came out from the one elf, its mouth not moving.

Wattie and Tunny stood there for a second, knew what they had to do, and teleported.

They came out at a lair, bugs scattered all along the walls, their backs shone green, their legs red. They started forward, until they came to an opening, and there she lay.

They prepared themselves and went for it. Charging forwards they went into the hole and started to attack her. They were killing her easy, their very strong swords, dragon, made light work of the queen. The knights kept on fighting, using shields to protect them. Suddenly Wattie shouted, 'Stand back.' He placed his sword in her, straight into her neck. She fell to the floor, a massive scream left her body, underneath lay it. The elf bow!

Matt Watkins (12)
Fair Oak Business & Enterprise College, Rugeley

The Enchantment Of Excalibur

Long ago there lived a boy called Arthur, he lived with a wizard called Merlin, who was Arthur's uncle. But Arthur didn't know that when he was born Merlin had cast a curse on him.

As of this day Arthur will find out about his curse. Arthur found a parchment which read: 'The only cure for Arthur's curse is to pull the Excalibur out of the sacred stone'. The rest of the parchment said: 'There's only one person who can pull it out, and if they do they become King of England'.

So Arthur set off on his adventure to Camelot where the sword was. Suddenly! Arthur saw a sword shimmer in the sunlight, so he ran over to it, so did 10,000 other people, to watch him of course. Arthur stepped up onto the stone and ripped his shirt off to show that he was strong. He pulled once, he pulled twice, he pulled the third time with a massive roar and out came the huge sword, and everybody cheered for him.

The next day the mayor announced Arthur, king, and the city of Camelot and King Arthur lived happily ever after.

Christopher Tunnicliffe (13)
Fair Oak Business & Enterprise College, Rugeley

The Vortex

Paul was a very shy child and didn't like to mix with anyone. The only things he felt comfortable with were his computer games. Whether it was PS2 or Xbox, you could guarantee within a week he would have completed it. He loved choosing games.

One day, a particular game caught his eye and he just had to buy it.

He got home and put it in his PS2 and started it up. He played until his thumbs went raw. When he got to level 20, a blue dot appeared. Paul ignored it. He had to play on. It got bigger until it filled the screen. Paul thought it would stop. It didn't. It got so big that it sucked him in.

He lay there floating in blue swirls just spinning around. Where was he? Paul panicked, until he realised that this place was familiar. He realised that he was in his game! He looked through the screen and noticed his mom was bringing up his tea. Paul started screaming until his mum finally heard him. She looked at the screen in horror and shouted, 'Paul, Paul, what shall I do?'

'Complete the level, quick!' bellowed Paul.

His mum was playing for ten minutes until: *Level completed, you win back your son!* Flashed on the screen. With a thud, Paul landed in his chair. When he did, his PS2 blew to bits!

Now Paul knows he's never going to play 'Final Destiny' again.

Christian Morden (13)
Fair Oak Business & Enterprise College, Rugeley

The Express Murder

It was a freezing cold night in Oakwood, the trees rustling in the midnight moonlight. There were two men walking past, the men quickly turned off into the dark, damp woods and started sprinting away.

I looked back towards Tesco Express and there was, lying in the middle of the road, a man with hundreds of bullets in his chest. Unbelievably, the man arose, and charged straight towards me hurling cars out of the way of his path. His face was dripping with blood, and his arms were hanging on by a thread.

He ran straight past me and ran through the way the two men went. All I heard after that were two screams and it went deadly silent for ages.

I quickly turned around and headed for Tesco. When I got there I scrambled up to the counter and managed to ring the police. When they arrived at the scene they found the bodies but there was no trace at all of the murderer. He left no signs, so they couldn't do anything, until one day a group of bike riders stumbled across a ditch which they looked in and found a body matching the description of the double murderer.

Nathan Hucks (13)
Fair Oak Business & Enterprise College, Rugeley

Dragon Slayer

There was a little girl named Zoey who lived in a castle in the middle of Fife. Zoey was forever wandering away from the castle grounds even after lots of warnings from her parents. Zoey's dad worked as a dragon slayer.

One day, Zoey was playing in the garden whilst her parents were having an afternoon cup of tea. They had just started drinking their tea when the doorbell rang. Zoey's dad answered the door. It was his friends telling him some bad news. The friend told him that there is another dragon in the village.

'Oh dear,' said the dragon slayer, 'I will search for him first thing tomorrow morning.'

In the meantime he realised Zoey had wandered off again. The family were frantic. He began his search immediately looking around the town, then he suddenly changed his direction and searched towards the cliffs to look for the dragon with the hope that his daughter would be found.

The dragon slayer was looking for the dragon for a good hour when he came across the dragon's cave. He crept inside the dangerous lair. He saw tons of blood splattered everywhere and instantly began to panic. Minutes later he saw his daughter safe but being teased by the dragon. He dived into the dragon, slayed him with his almighty sword and rescued his daughter. Then carried her home gently in his arms and from that day Zoey never wandered off again without her parents' permission.

Michael Padfield (13)
Fair Oak Business & Enterprise College, Rugeley

Life As A Tea Leaf

It was a warm spring morning in a tea field in China. I had just woken up and was very nervous because yesterday I had heard the farmers saying that they were going to collect their tea harvest in today. Oh no the farmers have arrived, what am I going to do?

'Argh!' I can get free from this plant.

'Noooooo!' Where am I? I must be in the back of a lorry. It's very noisy and bumpy. Then the lorry stopped.

Why are we being put in these bags with holes in the side? It looks similar to prison. 'Hey let me out I've done nothing wrong.'

Nobody answered. Then I started to move again. I shot down a tube and landed in a metal container. *Bang!*

Then the lid shut and everywhere went dark. Everyone else went to sleep. I never, though. I wanted to know where I was going. Our lorry began to move again. Then it stopped. It felt like we were being stacked. Then I got put in a basket, and whizzed along a beeper. It started to go bumpy again, so I thought that it must be in a car. Then it stopped. I got carried inside to find myself swimming in milk with sugar on my head. Then it started to get hot. They poured hot water all over me, spun me around with a metal thing, then picked me up and left me in a bin, where I finally died.

James Aucote (13)
Fair Oak Business & Enterprise College, Rugeley

The Worst Day Of My Life

It was the 12th May and we had just come back from fighting at the field. It had been a long, hard battle so far. As we were walking back to the campsite I heard someone shout, 'Everyone put their gas masks on.' As I was putting mine on I looked up to see that they were bombing us. I looked around to see if everyone had their gas masks on but someone didn't!

This young man was coughing like mad, drowning in the green sea of gas. His face pale like snow. He was staggering up to me when he fell to his knees, then to the floor. Blood and froth coming out of his mouth. As I ran up to him I found it was too late to save him. He was already gone.

A truck came along and two men came and threw him onto the back. They drove off and, as I was walking behind them, his body lay there motionless on the back of the truck, his head hanging over the edge. It was truly the worst day of my life. I will never forget the terrible thing that happened to this young man. Someone said he was only 18. He still had his whole life ahead of him.

Then I wondered what his family would feel like when they found out the devastating news.

Chloé Hunwick (12)
Fair Oak Business & Enterprise College, Rugeley

The Return Of The King

Long ago in the times of knights and wizards, there lived a man, who had no fear, a man who had never lost a battle, his name was Arthur. For many years he had been part of the Roman Empire with his loyal knights. As soon as the Roman Empire left Britain a new empire arrived and they were the Saxons.

For many years Arthur and Merlin (a magician with his tribe to try and change England back to its normal self) had been rivals, but when they heard about the Saxons, they decided to work together in a fight to drive away the Saxons.

As soon as they arrived at Hadrian's Wall, Arthur and his five loyal knights at his side were ready. The Saxons sent in a small group of soldiers to see what would happen. With no hesitation Arthur and his knights charged in with all their might. First charge, swords clattering and blood being shed. Second charge, same again. After five attacks they were all dead. Now it was time for the real challenge, the major army with about 1,000 soldiers. Everyone charged at full speed with anger. Arthur, his knights and Gwenivere leading Merlin's tribe against the Saxons. It was a bloody battle. After long hours of fighting Arthur came out victorious with deaths of a couple of his knights.

After that day peace had been restored to England with Arthur and Gwenivere becoming King and Queen of England.

Daniel Watson (12)
Fair Oak Business & Enterprise College, Rugeley

The Creature

It was midnight on a cold winter's night. Outside the snow covered the ground like a winter blanket. In the museum Mark had been on patrol. He was running through the museum looking for the nearest exit. He patrolled these corridors every day but somehow they seemed different in his panic. He suddenly felt like Jason in the labyrinth. He had been patrolling when he had heard a scream from inside one of the exhibits, when he looked he saw it, the creature that hunted him. It was standing over the other guard's body. It resembled a gargoyle it had horns coming out of its forehead. Massive ruby-red eyes and a long snake-like tail. The creature moved swiftly through the museum.

Mark had come to a dead end in the south wing. He had called the cops and told them about a robbery not the creature. Mark suddenly had a genius plan, he ripped the nearest painting off the wall. The alarm sounded and bars came down. He let out a sigh of relief and slumped victorious against the wall. Then he heard a footstep on the marble floor. Only then did he realise what he had done. The creature was locked inside with him. He heard police sirens outside but they were too late. All he could do was sit there and wait for death to take him.

Aaron Rawlinson (13)
Fair Oak Business & Enterprise College, Rugeley

Fairground Fright

My name is Joe, I am 15 years old. On the 16th of May 2006 I had a fairground accident, my best mate Jimmy died from this accident … this is how my story goes …

We were 150 feet high up in the sky on the best roller coaster in town. We were about to drop then all of a sudden we dropped in mid-air. My heart was racing. It was such a great feeling until I felt something come loose in my cart, I thought I was going to drop out then within a matter of seconds I hit the floor. *Bang!* I had fallen out of my cart.

From this moment I felt like I was dead. My best mate was dead, he was in the cart with me too, luckily for me I survived but unfortunately for him he sadly died.

The doctors said I'd had a lucky escape and didn't know how I'd survived it. They said I fought it all the way, but I fought it for Jimmy.

Six months later I came out of hospital. I came back blind in one eye and I was also in a coma for four months and I will not walk again.

Jimmy was the best mate you could ever have, a mate you could trust. I thought I could trust the fairground driver but I thought wrong. I'll never forget that day, it was the worst day of my life.

I wish I'd gone with Jimmy sometimes, I really do …

Laura Lindsay (13)
Fair Oak Business & Enterprise College, Rugeley

Deadly Dare

It was my dare, they chose me of all people! My bike's tyres had been punctured ... the faces of my friends were fading away.

I put my bike aside; it was tangled in nettles. I could no longer see anyone. It was all silent, all I could hear was the wind blowing softly giving a warm breeze. I was approximately four yards away from the door. My body was shivering as I moved closer.

I was so scared to go in there because nobody had been in there in donkeys' years, it was told that it was supposed to be haunted.

I reached out for the ancient hazel door, as I was about to push it, I heard a click. I looked around me, but there was nothing in sight. I looked down and all I saw was my dirty boots sunk in the mud: I looked up and through the window. I saw a dim light had been switched on.

I was dripping with perspiration. I once again reached for the door, I pushed it open and it made a loud creaky sound. I stayed outside, I looked through the open door, I could see nothing; just plain black. I decided a couple of minutes later that I would be confident and walk ahead. That's exactly what I did ... slowly.

I took a couple of steps until there was a ditch and I fell right down! The next thing I knew was that, I was lying in a bed next to other spirits that had set a trap for me to become one of them, they had succeeded! I was never to be seen again ...!

Shakila Chowdhury (12)
Fair Oak Business & Enterprise College, Rugeley

My Robotic Eye

It is the year 3000, and I am in school. I don't know how but I have skipped forward in time. My right eye has been replaced and everything I look at is green with a cross in the middle. I have a dark green robotic arm too, whenever I move it, it sounds like an electronic sunroof closing, and all of the teachers are holograms, controlled by the master.

The next day …

I was in literacy feasting on modern sweets called Fromaz's (similar to sticky toffee apples except bitesize).

'Johnathan, what are you eating?'

'Fromaz's.'

'You can't type with sticky fingers. To the master's office.'

I stood up quick and sharp, looked at her furiously and concentrated my energy onto her. My face was raging red. Looked her in the eye. *Bang!* She was gone. I don't know how I blew her up, it just happened.

Suddenly a speaker said, 'Johnathan Wood please report to the master's office.'

I dashed out of the room. The speakers kept on repeating. I sped round the corner, up the stairs. There was now a crowd of people following me. No one likes the master, he needs teaching a lesson.

I sped up another set of stairs at a rapid pace. Smashing open every door as I went. I was quicker than the speed of light.

I smashed his door open, I looked him in the eye. *Bang!* Serves him right for trying to control us. We're free from the master!

Neil Conway (13)
Fair Oak Business & Enterprise College, Rugeley

The Forgotten Painting

Tony, Rose and Jack were exploring in their new home, so Rose ran upstairs to see what she could find. When she got there she saw some old, rusting ladders leading to an attic. She scrambled up them and when she got there she saw an old, forgotten painting. On it was a farmer harvesting a field. She took it down to the first floor and hung it on the wall, turned around and headed back towards the attic, but before she could take another step, she had been sucked back towards the painting. The next thing she knew she was in it.

'Help! Help me!' she cried, starting to get worried. The farmer's tractor was coming closer towards her and even though she'd screamed her loudest the farmer couldn't hear her.

She heard Tony shout, asking her where she was. She couldn't see him, but answered anyway.

'I think I'm in a picture I found in the attic. It's on the wall next to my room!' Rose shouted with fear in her voice.

Tony saw the picture, so reached in to grab Rose, but struggled to pull her out. The tractor was only inches away when Jack appeared by Tony's side and helped him pull Rose free just in time to escape the tractor.

'Let's keep this our little secret, eh. Mum will never believe us,' Tony sighed, as they lay on the floor in shock.

Sarah Waring (13)
Fair Oak Business & Enterprise College, Rugeley

The Land Of Dreams

On Monday 8th May a long time ago a little girl named Lucy was fast asleep in her bed dreaming, but the dream she was dreaming was no ordinary dream. Lucy was dreaming about a land faraway, it had no name but Lucy knew that it was a very special and beautiful place.

So beautiful that it had clouds like cotton candy and, the rivers sparkled like diamonds.

Lucy couldn't wait to explore this magnificent land in her mind. She found herself on the top of a hill dotted with pretty little daisies, at the bottom ran the sparkling river with a little rowing boat bobbing up and down. It looked so inviting she couldn't keep herself from running down the hill and into the boat.

She picked up the oars and started to row down the stream. In the distance she could hear children playing, as she got closer she could hear them shouting, 'It's my turn.'

'No it's my turn.'

What could they be doing? She rowed faster and faster to see what the fuss was about.

Rubbing her eyes in disbelief No! It couldn't be. Was it? It was, it was the biggest whitest swan Lucy had ever seen, with wings as wide as the house she lived in and easily as tall. But that wasn't all, two children were sitting on the swan's back and taking it in turns to have the most wonderful ride flying round and round, and up and down on this beautiful creature. She rowed to the side of the riverbank and got out of her little boat.

This was just the very beginning of the most exciting adventure.

Lauren Carter (13)
Fair Oak Business & Enterprise College, Rugeley

An Hour In The Life Of ...

The ball is coming towards me, I hope it misses me! I really don't want to be hit, it really hurts. The ball skims the side of me. It's stopped by a person behind me. I can see the ball flying over me. I'm really scared.

It's so hot out here. It feels like my head is on fire! Oh no, I can see another ball coming towards me. It was hit high in the air and now there is a massive cheer. Something must have happened which was very pleasing. Now that the celebrations are over we can start again. More balls flying towards me.

I'm really pleased there is someone standing behind me. I don't think I could cope without them there. This person is saving my life most of the time! Another celebration, the person behind me has caught the ball. I'm so happy now because the person has saved my life yet again! I can't thank this person enough, I am so tense, I keep going from hot to cold, there must be something wrong with me.

Must not get hit, must not get hit, must not get hit. I keep thinking this over and over. The ball is coming towards me, I think this time it will hit me. It will hit me, it will, I'm so sure it will. The batter misses it. *Clunk,* ouch, that hurt. I just knew it was going to be hit. Everyone is celebrating apart from the batter.

Did you guess what I am ... ?

I'm a wicket in a cricket match.

Emma Travill (14)
Ferrers Specialist Arts College, Rushden

In An Angel's Life

She's running faster, as fast as her stick legs can take her, her heart begins to race. She stops, looks around then *smack,* she hits the floor.

'You really think you'd get away huh?'

Tilly looks up to see her nightmare, the girl picks her up by her long hair and begins punching Tilly's fragile body.

The rain pours onto Tilly as she lays there motionless. She wipes the blood off her face and begins to get up. She falls. She makes a second attempt, pain runs down her spine.

'I've had enough of my life, it's hell! At home and this endless bullying!' Tilly muttered to herself.

Tilly has been bullied ever since her, well … since I passed away, now I'm worried she will follow in my footsteps …

Tilly runs up the stairs when she gets home. now she's in my room looking for something. I dread what it is …

She writes …

'Mum I am sorry to put you through this. but I've had enough of my life! Since I was little you hit me, beat me black and blue. I hate the school bullies, I hate it with you, Mum. I will still love you unlike you loved me. I hope this hits your heart, Mum, I really do! How are you going to feel when I'm not here, Mum? Mum, this really hurts, watching this happen to my body. Goodbye, Mummy. Love Tilly xxx

I watch … I begin to cry.

Rebekah Byer (14)
Ferrers Specialist Arts College, Rushden

Bright Lights

He stumbled through another seedy back alley, trying to find what he was looking for. He had done the same for months before. Each day he couldn't find what he sought, he felt as though he were letting her down.

The bright lights of the city seemed a million miles away, the guiding lights of home were gone. He slid down the side of the dumpster to the cold, hard floor. Reaching into his suit pocket he pulled out what was once a note, but was now nothing more than a tear-soaked piece of scrap paper.

The neon lights of the clubs glowed on eerie blue, the blue of her eyes. Even over the smell of his cheap cologne he could still smell her sweet perfume.

'Keep thinking,' she whispered softly in his ear. Her golden locks flowed across his shoulder.

Once again he raised the whiskey bottle to his mouth. 'I'll try,' and with one swig she was gone.

Alex Rudgalvis (14)
Ferrers Specialist Arts College, Rushden

A Day In The Life Of A Roll Of Masking Tape

I start my day like any other, shoved in the dark, gloomy drawer. No friends, no life, just the drawer …

There I was, daydreaming, when suddenly a small hand reached for me. The light was too bright. Part of me was cut off, and as you can imagine, it really hurt. Turns out I was repairing a relationship, via photograph. Something bad was going to happen, I could tell. I had that feeling.

He soon finished with me, chucking me straight back into my empty, lonely drawer. The mouldy smell of gardening gloves overpowered me.

Hours later, an enormous hand grabbed me. *What now?* I thought to myself, *Not again!* this was one of the worst. I've never done anything this terrible in my life. What has become of me? Letting this horrible, horrible thing happen! So here goes. He cuts me, harder than ever, the force is killing me. I'd rather die than do this though, I'm sure anyone would.

I can hear the young one crying, screaming, and telling him to stop. I get put on the lips of the young one, and the rest of me is thrown on the floor. Can anything be worse than this torture he and I are both going through? It all goes silent. The young one stops weeping, and I stop breathing …

Here's the end.

Rebecca Mantle (14)
Ferrers Specialist Arts College, Rushden

The Journey Of The Photo Frame

I really like where I am, above the mantle of the fireplace, it is lovely and warm and has a great view, just perfect for a nosy photo frame like myself. But I must soon get a repaint. I can feel the rust growing out through my frame, though luckily I heard the lord and lady booking my beauty appointment (as I like to call it). I love the affection I get when being repainted, just heavenly, as if I were a pampered angel ... but I do wonder what happens with the jewels behind me as I go to be repainted; they all get awfully lonely by themselves - poor babies.

Wow! This place has really changed since last time I came, it is now even better than any frame I could imagine, I can't wait to tell the girls. I do love the fresh sensation once finished, I feel young and beautiful, especially with those gorgeous jewels behind me.

Hours have passed since my repaint, I told the jewels about my experience and the mirror and the ornament and well, everyone! But it's getting late and the curtains have closed themselves tight which means it must be time for my beauty sleep. But just then as I started to drift off into a deep sleep, the lady walks in tense and nervous, stuttering and staggering, but trying to act bravely.

'I haven't stolen the jewels!' she backs against the wall, frightened, as a tall, dark man draws out his blood-covered dagger. He is mad with the lady and points it up by her chin keeping close eye contact and just as the lady takes a large gulp, he swings the dagger and stabs her several times in the chest. I quickly shield the jewels' eyes as it is much too gory for them.

Shocked and worried, the surroundings and I sit in horror staring at the dead body. Then suddenly two men in uniform barge into the lord and lady's house. Madmen like beasts rampage through the blood-covered scene but I don't understand why.

After a period of total destruction one of the men throws me to the ground. My glass is smashed and my heart broken as they walk out in relief with my babies, the jewels disappear with no effort.

Holly Smith (14)
Ferrers Specialist Arts College, Rushden

An Hour In The Life Of ...

I watched his face as my point pierced his pale, blotchy skin. He pushed my singular long arm down, and allowed the deadly liquid to flow into his veins. His bloodshot eyes rolled back in his head. He lay there stiff and motionless, like a plank of rotting wood. I slid downwards slowly, from his thin stick-like wrist and lay there, still, on the draughty dust-covered floor.

Was I really a cold-blooded murderer?

I hate seeing this happen. I feel terribly guilty, despite the fact that this whole process is practically out of my control. I don't feel as if it's me that does it, I suppose it's some sort of subconscious thinking or something.

Another man entered the room, he saw his friend laying there, pale-faced and blue-fingered, he looked cold and lifeless. The man ran from the room and searched distressed for the phone. He dialled the numbers, *beep, beep, beep.*

'Hello! ... Hello?' ... he stammered rushing the person on the receiving end of the phone.

'Hello ... yes hello it's about my friend,' he said reluctantly. 'I think he might be ... dead!' And then ... a terrible feeling of guilt struck in ...

... a syringe.

Rachel Wharwood (14)
Ferrers Specialist Arts College, Rushden

A Day In The Life Of ...

Crunch! There goes my head. *Crunch!* There goes the right side of my body. *Crunch!* There goes the left side of my body. He decided he didn't want the rest of me. He chucked me away like I was nothing. All that was left of me was my meaty middle. My eyes closed.

I woke up feeling soggy from the rainy night. I looked around. A seagull way up high was hovering. *Swoop!*

This will be a quick way to dry. I can see everything from up here. While I was flying in this very uncomfortable beak I could think about what I was going to do to find the rest of my body parts.

Argh! My last bit of lettuce was falling out of me. In the beak I found a long bit of stringy grass. I kept hold of it. Suddenly a blast of wind came through the beak and made the grass attach to the lettuce. I pulled it in and shoved it back into me. *That's better!* I thought to myself. I saw a girl burger from way up high. I shouted to the bird, 'Let me down!'

'Cor, cor,' he replied.

I guessed that meant okay. He dropped me.

I thought twice about talking to the girl. She wouldn't look twice at me but I thought wrong. She turned around and I noticed that she had had a bite out of her head. She was my missing piece.

Megan Williams (14)
Ferrers Specialist Arts College, Rushden

An Hour In The Life Of ...

She carries me round everywhere. To the shops, to school, out with her friends. Always pressing my buttons. It tickles! I love it when I sing, I light up like the stars!

We're going shopping today, can't wait. She might buy me a new outfit. Ooo, I'm singing! It's Chelsey.

'Hey!' I say with joy, 'You coming out?'

'Brianna replies, 'No, sorry mate, I'm going shopping to get some new jeans.'

Disappointed I say, 'OK, bye!' Brianna putts me in her handbag ready to go.

We wait at the bus stop for five minutes for the bus to arrive. Brianna jumps on, pays for a ticket and off we go. Where shall we sit? *Uh-oh* I hear those boys. I hate those boys, they're always causing trouble. This can't be good. I'm scared. I don't want them to hurt Brianna.

We sit down. She's unzipping her bag. Finally, some light. She gets me out. I see the boys two rows behind. Brianna opens me up. She starts picking through her photos. Ooo, that's my favourite. She has her hair in beautiful curls flowing down her shoulders. With her eyes, such a gorgeous shade of green. Eyelashes so long, fluttering like butterflies.

She puts me back in her handbag. It's our stop. Wait, the bus is moving again. Has Brianna missed her stop? Oh no, she can't have done. She's left me on the bus! This is horrible! The bag is shaking. The boys, they've got me and *smash!* There I go all over the floor.

This is an hour in the life of a mobile phone.

Beth Pearman (13)
Ferrers Specialist Arts College, Rushden

My Life, The Life Of A Knife

Is it me that's in the wrong? I have no choice but I have been captured. I wish I could fight back. But I can't.

They scream. I jab into their body, once, twice, three times. Now they are dead. That was the third, only two more to go.

I am put down. My owner drinks a strange liquid, he picks me up and runs. Then we stop.

I can't take it anymore! I won't do it! She is only five, a dark alley, a man with a weapon. *No!* I try to scream but nothing happens, nobody hears me! *Jab!* Now, she is dead.

My owner laughs. How dare he? I try to hurt him but I am clasped in his grip, unable to move. He moves over to the green bin in the corner, opens the lid, drops me inside. My bloodstained body falling deeper and deeper. *Crash!* I have hit the bottom. I am embedded in rubbish, stuck here for days.

One day, nothing. Two days, nothing. Three days, a light, the bin is opening. I am picked up. No! I must stay, stay in my dark hole of a grave, I killed them. OK I killed them! I am a knife and I killed them!

Laura Kirkup (13)
Ferrers Specialist Arts College, Rushden

An Hour In The Life Of The Witness

I am the witness. The only witness. Staring day after day, night after night. I am the only one who knows exactly what happened. Do you?

I saw him. I saw what he did. Nobody else did. I saw the pain on his face and the anger of another. I saw the shiny object glisten in the moonlight.

I've seen some horrible things in my long life but nothing this shocking. He fell to the floor like a lead balloon. I saw it from start to end. He didn't know I was there.

They were running, running away from each other. They stopped beneath me. Shouting at each other, pointing, spitting and pushing. One of them, tall, dark hair called by the name of John and the other named Winston, he was black, he was average height, dark hair.

The tall white man revealed a shiny object, he started to wave it around pointing it towards Winston, still shouting aggressively telling him to go back home to where he is from. Then suddenly he punched Winston violently with the knife, Winston recoiled and hit the floor.

He laid there still. John laughed and walked away, proud of what he had done. He thought no one had seen what he had done, well that's what he thought.

I saw what happened. I saw what he did, although I cannot stop it. I am the witness, the only witness.

Katie Jackson (14)
Ferrers Specialist Arts College, Rushden

An Hour In The Life Of ...

Beep beep 10.58pm ... I'm guarding the house while the family is out. But what was that? *Zoom!* It was dark, it was hard to notice what that image was! It was creeping towards the front door. I was tracking him into the house. Oh no, he has just walked in, what can I do? All I've got to do is look inside somewhere, trying not to make it too obvious. The family will be nearly home, at least I'm a witness to the police. Where has he gone? I'm looking in all the rooms, zooming in and everything. I hope the image hasn't gone outside. I hope he hasn't gone upstairs. I can't reach up there.

Wait, the family has just turned up into the driveway. The image is still in the house, he is in the front room. Argh! What do I do? What do I do? ... All I have got to do is watch what the image is doing, and to record it in my head. Oh no! The mum of the house has left her jewels on the tiny table under the lamp. Hopefully the image won't notice them. Here comes the family, they've turned the light on.

'Argh!' screams Mum. Ouch, that hurt my microphone. I see that image ... is a nasty burglar.

'At least he hasn't taken my jewels,' Mum says under her breath. Then the nasty burglar notices them out of the corner of his eye and grabs the jewels. Then suddenly he rushes out of the open door. I am following him all the way to see which way he rushes off to. *Beep beep ... 11.58pm.*

... a CCTV camera!

Robyn Hoddell (13)
Ferrers Specialist Arts College, Rushden

An Hour In The Life Of …

I have no sympathy for her, it's over. It's gone quiet, she turns my music on. It's dark, I'm in her pocket, I think. She's walking. *Crack!* I'm on the floor. I can hear footsteps, they're running. I can see a man, where is my owner? I'm ringing, the man stops, and *crack!* I'm on the floor again. I can hear her, she's screaming, her mum's talking, she says she was mugged. I have no feelings, her mum is crying. It's silence.

I'm in her pocket and she is walking again, everything has stopped. I'm awake and in her bedroom, I can see birds, birds flying past the window, singing to themselves. The trees are swaying in the wind.

She opens the window, *bang!* It's all red, where has she gone? What's happened? I hear noises, someone's shouting and screaming.

A man is climbing through the window, he's picked me up, where is he taking me, he's pressing my buttons, I'm ringing. *Crack!* I'm on the floor again, my button has broken. The man's lying on the floor.

I'm confused. I have no feelings or emotion about what's going on. It's gone dark.

I've been asleep for ages, I'm awake again, where am I? I've got a new owner, ooh, who's he? He's cute. Must be her new boyfriend. He looks unhappy, he says it's over.

Ooh no this is gonna happen again, I don't want to go through it all again. I have no feelings, but it hurts and confuses me. I'm dead.

Kirstie Hawthornthwaite (13)
Ferrers Specialist Arts College, Rushden

An Hour In The Life Of A … ?

Staring, yes, all of them are staring at me. My family and I! They all look similar, but very different. I run for my mother but I can't find her. It's just Dodo and me. In a small room. With lots of toys. I remember my mum. I saw her yesterday. I've never been here before.

Oh!

Flashback

No! It can't be! Those beasts took my mother away! But then that other strange thing helped me and fed me …

Hang on! Here he is again, with more food and water! No wait! I remember!

Flashback

Me, my family and my friends were running. I heard a loud noise. It sounded like a bang! My friend fell straight to the ground. *Bang!* And down went another. Every bang another one fell. Another louder bang and my mum was gone, that's when I hid! I was scared! Ouch. Oh no they got me!

It's hard to remember. It's coming back to me though. Dodo is having a drink and he's on the rope. The beast has finally left! Wait!

Flashback

I woke up in a big cage. My friends too but I could not see or hear my mum. We were on a very bumpy road but we stopped! The beasts came over and stabbed something sharp in me!

I woke up in this place! This iron prison! This hellhole! But I don't understand. The beasts are feeding me well and I am perfectly healthy, but why is everyone staring and pointing at me? Hang on! I think … No it can't be … I have heard of these places … a … zoo! I'm a monkey in a zoo!

Harry Fletcher (14)
Ferrers Specialist Arts College, Rushden

An Hour In The Life Of …

Kerching! The sound of the till opening up, coins rattle, pound notes rustling like leaves on a tree on a windy day waiting to fall.

Kerching! The noise goes again only this time … Oh no! I'm being pulled out of the till, why me? Why me? What have I done? I'm only a £10 note minding his own business.

Oh great! Now I am in a pocket, it's so dark, it's like a small narrow room with no air to breathe, and *phewee!* What a stench.

But wait, there is a hole nearby. If I can get there then I might be able to escape, anyway here goes *allee oomph!*

Yes I am free but what do I do? Where can I go?

What! Not again! Here comes another bumpy ride, *whoosh!* I've been blown away. *'Argh!'*

Woah! That was close and now it's raining but luckily I'm protected from the rain and *huh* I feel tired *huh huh!* Hey where am I? Ah what, not another pocket. It's just like jumping through time or to another planet but with no way of seeing it happen, and oh great it smells like a pig has just lived here.

Ding-dong! Ding-dong! Hey I know that sound, that sounds like the door of a sweet shop and hooray! I'm back in a till again … Hang on, uh-oh here we go again. *'Argh!'*

Martin Burke (15)
Ferrers Specialist Arts College, Rushden

What Am I?

I am cold, so so cold. Why am I here? I'm in a cage, I can't move a muscle, not a muscle. Days I've been sitting here.

Oh no, the cage is falling. *Bang!* Things are falling on top of me, what if the cage breaks? I'll be crushed. I'm moving again. A long red light has beamed across my face with a loud *beep!* I am being shaken and rattled then ... darkness. I can hear voices and more rumbling. I feel a lot warmer now, but as soon as I feel warm I am just as cold as before.

Weeks I have been here, alone, counting sheep ... 1345 ... 1346 ... 1347. Wait I can see light and finally the cage has been opened. I can feel a rush of air on my face, like I was standing on a huge cliff overlooking a vast ocean. I feel free like I could run for miles and miles. However, with my new-found sense of freedom I cannot feel the immense pain of burning fire. I can smell my flesh and my skin sizzling. I am flipped onto my face. I try to get up but I am forced back down, my face is burning, boiling, someone please *help me!* I am stuck between two soft things and liquid is being poured onto my wounds. I think that someone is trying to help me. How foolish of me. Oww! Someone has just taken a big bite out of me and I am plunging down a dark, dank, dismal hole.

What am I ... ? A hamburger!

Jason Peace (14)
Ferrers Specialist Arts College, Rushden

An Hour In The Life Of A Football!

You don't know how much it hurts getting kicked about so much. It's the finals tomorrow. Oh no! even more pain. Why oh why do I have to be a football, out of all the things? *Argh!* I hate my life!

It's so unfair, tomorrow they're going to kick lumps out of me.

Well … here I am sitting here alone in the park waiting for my owner, David, to come back from the shop.

Oh, here he comes now.

Wait, that's not David, it's Ryan, the school bully, and he's walking right up to me!

Argh! They're taking me with them.

It's times like this that I just wish people could hear what I'm saying. Well David isn't exactly going to get me back off of Ryan is he?

This can't be actually happening, I've been with David my whole life, since I was first pumped up!

I can see my whole life running before me, I'll probably get kicked over some random fence and I'll never be retrieved. Heck they might put the blade in me! David would never treat me like that.

They're playing football with me now!

Wait! I've got one brilliant idea … if I can roll my way each time they kick me hard then maybe David will come back and see me!

Ryan being the big clodhopper that he is has kicked me in the bush! Good one!

Yes! It's David, he's running, he must have noticed.

Come on David, come on! My amazing idea worked and I haven't even got a brain, how about that!

Cameron Bower (13)
Ferrers Specialist Arts College, Rushden

An Hour In The Life Of ...

I'm 350 years old. I stand tall and watch over the land. Every day I wake I see a brother of mine gone and just a stump on the ground. I think to myself, *am I next?* Ouch! Ouch! Ouch! That hurt my toe as it feels like an itch on a leg, the wind picks up as I fall to the floor.

'Timber!' someone says as I slam onto the cold floor. They chop off all my legs, my hair, my arms and take me in a van to a factory.

It's big and grey in every single way, I'm off, moving again, I'm moving on a belt towards a big sharp saw. Then it shreds me in little pieces. A4, A3, A5 and more, nice and thin and white. I can't move a thing. I'm as light as a feather then placed in a small brown box. Wait I know this box, it looks familiar. Wait, 'Brother is that you?' But nothing, it's not, not a single word, I sigh and just lie still in this dark, dark box with nothing to do just laying on myself.

Then, ha, ha, ha, that tickles, I'm all blue now. I'm all in a ball then in a brown bin, then in a black bag, then thrown. Thrown on a boat then, *rip* I'm caught by a man, a tall man then put in a green box. I'm moved and moved and moved again. I come back nice and clean, then in a small brown box, wait, I know this box. 'Brother is that you?' No, no, it isn't, then I'm off, off again and written on again. Wait, I can read, the title says: 'An hour in the life of ... ' of what? Of what? I'll read it and find out, oh I know who it is, it's me! It's me! I'm famous. *Cough, cough, cough* I can't talk that much ... I think something's coming on ... I ... !

James Neagle (14)
Ferrers Specialist Arts College, Rushden

An Hour In The Life Of …

As I crept around the corner of the pub I noticed a tall, dark figure emerging through the fog of the night. As it came towards me I felt colder and colder, but I dared not move or even breathe, and let the steam (due to all the coldness) come out of my mouth. The light from inside the pub was glaring and made it difficult to see how near it was to me. From behind me I could hear the Bolero music blaring in my eardrums. As a taxi drew up to the front of the pub I could just make out the figure of a man, he was wearing a long pair of ripped jeans and a navy blue hoodie.

'Ca' I giv' ya a lif' lil' ma'e?' he asked me.

He picked me up and I let out a bark. I licked his face and snuggled into him. He walked over to the taxi and placed me on a blanket on the front seat and drove away.

It wasn't the most pleasant of journeys home but at least I was warm and safe … Well, that's what I thought until *screech!* This was a sound that I recognised. I knew I was in some sort of danger, so I jumped up and stared out of the window. I saw a car spinning out of control, and there were horns blowing everywhere. I couldn't watch because I was too scared, I closed my eyes, then … *bang!* Everything went dark …

Hannah Edwards (13)
Ferrers Specialist Arts College, Rushden

My Dream Comes True

At first I am stuck at the back of the locker, crowded by boots, shirts, canes and dust. The caretaker walks into the room looking for me. Finally my dream is coming true. He opens the locker door … In a rush he throws everything out, finally I can see daylight. He picks me up and says, 'It's time,' then all of a sudden I'm flying through the air in his hands as he runs through the corridor, up the stairs and into the ground.

I look to see what's in front of me, I see the most amazing thing ever, 52,000 Geordies cheering the words. 'Newcastle United' He throws me towards the centre of the pitch, then all of a sudden I am rolling around the pitch, but as I am rolling towards a Newcastle player, he lobs me over another player's head.

I lands at the feet of *Alan Shearer*. He looks up then looks at me, then *bang!* he kicks me so hard towards goal. I think to myself, *I'm in* as I fly past the net. As I spin around I see 52,000 Geordies on their feet whilst Alan Shearer runs to the corner to celebrate.

Alan runs towards me and picks me up as if I am the World Cup. He kisses me and runs back to the centre of the pitch, still all I can hear is the fans chanting Shearer's name, that is the best sound I have ever heard.

Aaron Gilson (14)
Ferrers Specialist Arts College, Rushden

The Masked Man

Bang! 'Who, what, where, when?' said a dazzled 13-year-old teenager called Jordan Zepherlump. It was only a bolt of lightning and a short rumble of thunder.

Then the lights dimmed. 'Quiet Ralf, stop barking,' said a half asleep teenager. Then all of a sudden, a loud thud shook the whole house.

'Oww!' said a groany voice from somewhere downstairs. It said it again, so Jordan grabbed his torch and made his way to the top of the stairs. As nervous as he was he started to tiptoe down the stairs.

He got to the bottom of the stairs. His heart was going 20 to the dozen. He heard the noise again, it sounded like it came from the kitchen. He flicked on the torch as he shone it around the hallway. As he shone the torch around, he caught something that reflected the beam. It moved closer, then there was a strange whimper, fortunately Jordan recognised the sound. It was his dog, Ralf. He called him and Ralf came bounding over. 'Quiet dog,' said Jordan in a hushed voice. They both carried on down the hallway, towards the kitchen.

They got to the kitchen. Jordan peered round the corner. He saw to his amazement two legs waving around in the air. The voice said again, 'Help me, help me!' With his dog by his side, Jordan walked up to the cupboard where the figure lay ...

Scott Winfrow (14)
Ferrers Specialist Arts College, Rushden

An Hour In The Life Of ...

Reapplying me one more time. Then it happened. How could she not see him? He was right behind her. He was slowly creeping up on her. He raised his hand clutching a sharp object. She saw his reflection in the mirror. She screamed a piercing sound; she ran into the street, she dropped me! *Stomp, stomp, stomp* suddenly a sharp halt. I was picked up by a hot, sweaty hand. It was him! He lifted me and dropped me into a dark, warm hole. I was rolling around for hours.

He reached in, *bang,* he slammed me on the table, there was a man on the floor with a red hole in his chest. Was he *dead*? He had her. He had her locked in a room without any windows. He dragged her out and frantically tied her to a chair. He held me in one hand and a gun in the other. She's my owner, I can't let him hurt her!

He kept asking her questions! She didn't answer. I saw in her eyes she was so, so afraid. What can I do? I can't move! I can't yell! He shouted and said he had no choice! Was this really happening? I heard a slow steady movement. With his last ounce of energy he reached for his penknife and cut him in his main artery. He bled to death. He untied her. She grabbed me, her soft, warm hands. She reapplied me again, hopefully not for the last time.

An hour in the life of a ... lipstick.

Bailey Helsdown (13)
Ferrers Specialist Arts College, Rushden

Broken Dreams

Sitting in the corner, still holding the Zopiclone, I watched her. She was spread out on the floor. Her greasy blonde hair and baggy clothes surrounding her. Her face looked weary. Beside her hand was an empty glass, and beside that an empty bottle. The living room was messier than usual. Cans of Stella and empty packets of food were covering the carpet. The smell was unbearable.

She was motionless. But I didn't feel pain. I didn't feel scared that maybe she was gone. I wasn't upset. Just numb, like the feelings I had for her. I knew she never loved me. She was incapable of love. All she was capable of was drinking and smoking. I felt relieved that maybe I'd finally get to go to a home where people cared. Where families sat at the table, and discussed their day. Where parents nagged at their children to do their homework. I was thinking that maybe I would get a brother or a sister and maybe share a room. Maybe we would fight over toys or whose turn it was to sit in the front. If I was lucky I might even get a goodnight kiss or if God had suddenly answered my prayers, I'd get a bedtime story.

I had never experienced a normal family. Whatever that was. Suddenly she stirred and all my dreams floated away. I regretted that the woman I couldn't call my mother, was still alive.

Nicola Ashington (14)
Granville Community School, Swadlincote

Jack

The boy was sprawled out over the damp mattress on the floor. He was like a dead body, motionless, not moving, just a little quiver as a small Jack Russell slid his nose against the boy's pale face.

Still he didn't move.

He was surrounded by empty Carling cans and used Budweiser bottles. Still the small dog tried to wake his weak, pitiful owner up.

Jack was a little Jack Russell but had a big heart and loved his owner, his drunk, half-drugged, knocked-out owner.

After about an hour or two, the drunk, half-witted slob got up and reached for another can of Carling and sat back down as if everything was normal. But Jack knew for sure it wasn't.

A year ago that young boy was a good citizen, in college, great job, brilliant wage, but now he was out of his job, kicked out of college and on the run for dealing drugs. That perfect life and his wonderful wage thrown away on alcohol and his heroin addiction. All that perfect life thrown away by Shaun Price.

But why? Shaun was loved by everyone, but now all he had was a small dog called Jack.

Scott Barnett (14)
Granville Community School, Swadlincote

Lost Somewhere

I was sitting not knowing where I was. What had happened to me, where was I, how was I going to get home?

I looked around. It was dark, there was only one window, all I could see was the moon out of the top of it. All of a sudden I heard a door unlocking. I couldn't see the door, then out of nowhere a man was standing in the light, I couldn't look at him, it was too bright, the man shut the door, he turned a light on, it was dim.

I could see more now, not much but some more. I asked the man where I was, he didn't reply. The man started to walk over to me; I got to my feet, he told me to sit. There we were, both sitting in the dark, it seemed like hours, but as I looked at my watch only ten minutes had passed.

I kept thinking over and over what was going to happen to me, who was this man? It was getting late; it was almost two in the morning.

The man left the room but all he said to me was, 'I'll come and see you again tomorrow, you should get some sleep.'

I lay down on the floor, it was cold, it was damp. I closed my eyes, I could see my mum, I could see my dad, I slowly fell off to sleep, I was happy now, I felt safe.

Natasha Williams (14)
Granville Community School, Swadlincote

Imprisoned By My Mother

I sat on the splintering chair, sleepy and motionless, waiting for something terrible to happen. I heard the door creakily open, beads of sweat slowly dripped from my paralysed face. I tried to breathe, I shrieked as loudly as I could but it came out so quiet it was almost a whisper.

A woman slowly paced her way towards me. She had straggly pitch-black hair, skin as white as a cloud, she had black make-up around her evil eyes, blood-red lipstick surrounded her yellow pointy teeth. Snakes and pythons hung around her skeletal body. She cackled when she saw my terrified face.

I focused my eyes and realised this gothic woman was my mother, the evil woman who beat me as a child, always had a reason to be disappointed in me. I ran from her, now she had found me.

'You can run but you can't hide,' she said in her voice of death.

Those words were familiar from when I'd hid under my bed and in my wardrobe.

'I'm never a person to let a punishment slip,' she whispered, her voice drifting through the air like poisonous venom.

She removed the snakes and pythons from her neck, and draped them around me. A large one circled my neck and began to choke me. I saw my mother's evil grin as everything started to go black, I couldn't breathe. I saw a bright light and that was it, I was dead.

Stacey Jewell (13)
Granville Community School, Swadlincote

Tornado

The shutters creaked and slammed against the window, people screaming faintly in the distance. It was to this they awoke: Lucy and Steven rushed up out of bed, quickly got changed and ran downstairs. The screaming got louder. The shutters were beginning to come off their hinges. Steven opened the front door slowly, but as he opened it about two inches more the door flew open and a powerful gust of wind took Lucy's breath away. Lucy was in shock but carried on to walk outside with her partner, Steven.

'Help me, I'm trapped, I can't get out,' screamed a lady's voice.

At this moment Lucy and Steven looked in the direction of the screaming voice and were horrified to see some of the neighbourhood flattened.

All of a sudden there was an eerie calm around them, together they looked straight above them into the sky and all they could see was a circle of clear blue sky, this was obviously the eye of the tornado, or had they not survived and was this their pathway to Heaven?

Lucy awoke to the sound of the telephone ringing!

This was in fact the most realistic dream that Lucy had ever had.

When Lucy finally answered the phone it was her mother asking if they were OK as she had heard on the news a tornado had hit Lucy's village.

So was it a dream or reality? Lucy was too scared to look outside to see if there was any damage.

Kelly Lawrence (14)
Granville Community School, Swadlincote

Escape!

'I've got to leave him,' I said.

'I know, Meg,' said my best friend, Laura.

My so-called boyfriend Henry has beaten me twice. What if he beats my daughter, Lucee?

I remember packing a lot of things. Laura suggested that I stay with Lucee's dad. That would be weird. I put the bags in my car. I got in, it was half past two. Laura went to fetch Lucee. Henry came in and went to bed. I collected some more things, then told Lucee to get in the car.

'Mum, where are we going?' she asked.

'Dad's house, well you are.' I replied.

We got to Kyle's house and knocked. He answered, took one look at me and we went inside. 'Meg, did he do this to you?' he asked.

'Dad, I'm tired,' said Lucee.

'Come on, me and Mum will be up to read a story,' he replied.

Lucee climbed the silent stairs up to her room.

'Yes,' I said when Lucee had gone.

Knock, knock.

'Megan, Megan, get out here!' screamed Henry.

'Meg, go to Lucee and ring the police,' Kyle said.

Terrified, I ran upstairs. I just wanted to be safe. I rang and explained to the police everything. They came with an ambulance. Kyle was bleeding badly.

Henry got arrested, we went to court. He pleaded not guilty to assault on me and Kyle, but he got sentenced, three years in prison.

I was being stalked, whoever it was, they had killed me and my family. Someone who knew Henry wanted revenge. They got it.

Natalie Thomas (13)
Granville Community School, Swadlincote

Game Over!

The crimson sun beat down on my bare head, scorching my already burning arms. I could not walk this desert in my shoes; I would have to take them off. I placed my exposed flesh onto the inferno-like sand. It felt as if I was walking on flaming coals. My mouth was sandpaper; someone could light a match off my tongue.

I thought I was going to dwindle into nothing in this fiery wasteland and join the bones immersed in the sand. In the distance, what was it? Three men. This had to be a mirage, but I passed out before I got a chance to see them.

When I awoke I was in some kind of Aboriginal tent. I could tell this because of the ornaments surrounding the tent edge. This place was new to me and I was afraid to leave, to see the outside world.

A person entered and asked me to come and meet the rest of his tribe. He seemed nice so I did so. The tribe stared at me with a look of hunger in their eyes. Suddenly I felt a sharp pain in my back. I had been stabbed. These people were cannibals. This was the end. Game over!

That was my life. I've had enough of this. Time to get a new virtual reality game.

Tyla Houlton (14)
Granville Community School, Swadlincote

Runaway Hitchhiker

Clenched fists, opening then closing, unnerving eyes burning into me.

Blood gushing from my mother's open wound. Streaming down her cold body. Her clothes saturated with her own blood. Laying on the floor, sprawled out across the wooden ground, as her body began to make a stench.

I nervously turned my head towards the motionless man in front of me. The man I used to happily call my father. No facial expression whatsoever. Nothing.

Without thinking I snatched the cellphone from on top of the varnished unit and automatically ran for the large oak door.

Locking the door behind me, I heard fast heavy boots following. Putting my head to the door listening carefully, a thud shimmied the door, making it shake so vigorously, that I almost banged my head as I jolted backwards.

Pushing the buttons so hard and fast, my fingers began to get sore.

He was getting so angry and upset. I thought he was going to break down the solid, almost unbreakable door. Suddenly I unclamped my hands, dropped the cell phone and started to pull at the window.

So impatient I grabbed the lamp adjacent to my bed and smashed it into the glass, with so much force, I sliced my index finger as I did so. I pulled myself out of the hole.

Shimmying down the broken drainpipe, running across the half mown lawn, then sprinting down the lane and into the road. A car halted in front of me, throwing the passengers out of their seats, flagging me in. I hurried for the door as if he were behind me.

At last they drove away and I secretly gave a little smile.

Jodie Litchfield (14)
Granville Community School, Swadlincote

Dangerous Water

As I swam through the dark, dirty, dangered sea there was some rustling that I heard below. It was like it smelt my fresh blood. I'd cut my foot on ancient fossil that's what it felt like down under. I tried my hardest not to hesitate. I pulled my goggles down and looked. It was all black as if I were in a dark tunnel. But I did see a shadow that was darker than the sea. I couldn't make out what it was though.

I swam from the water as quickly as I could. I grabbed my belongings and told my friend, Aaron, to run and we hid behind a palm tree. The creature must have been amphibious because it was also running on land. The look of this was indescribable.

Aaron said to me, 'What's happening?'

I whispered, 'Be quiet!'

Everyone had left the beach. I peeked round the tree and there was no sign of it. I and Aaron went back to the hotel.

Later on the next day Aaron and I went back to the beach. We went to go on a boat and we didn't think that the creature would be back. So we risked it. The boat had a slide, so I went down it. At that moment something grabbed my leg, it was that monster and I was gone!

'Aaron that game was good, can we play that another time?'

'Yes course we can,' said Aaron.

Kirsty Griffiths (14)
Granville Community School, Swadlincote

Something Is Lurking!

On Hunter Street twin girls, Rose and Pansy, and their younger brother, Oliver, were on their way home from school. It was a lovely hot summer's day and they were all sweating so they decided to call in at a house to see if they could have a drink, as it was quite a walk from their own home.

'Can I pick the house we go to please?' asked Oliver.

'If you must!' said Rose sarcastically. So that was it. Oliver was going to choose the house they visited. They walked along the streets and Oliver was gazing around him choosing.

'Hurry up! I'm really thirsty you know,' moaned Pansy, holding her throat.

Oliver turned round unexpectedly and shouted, 'That one!'

Pansy and Rose looked round in shock to see a crooked little wooden house, if that's what you could call it. It wasn't a very nice looking place as its shutters were hanging off and the door had holes in it.

'Very well,' said Rose in disgust. They walked to the door, which fell down as they knocked. A deep laugh broke out and the three children wanted to run but they knew that they couldn't. They stepped into the house, the floorboards creaked. The laugh broke out again. Oliver screamed and then turned and ran. Pansy and Rose who were so shocked, followed him.

The three children never had their drink in the end. I wonder what was lurking in the old wooden house?

Gemma Bark (13)
Granville Community School, Swadlincote

Angry Dog

Angry Dog was an angry dog. He was always angry at something, even when he got all he wanted. He hated everyone and everything. He once went on a hunger strike because the price of eggs was too high! He doesn't even eat eggs! He barely even looks at them!

One day, while Angry Dog was moaning under his breath about something that he didn't like, Rover the Rottweiler asked him a question.

'Angry?' he asked. 'Why are you always so angry?'

'Go away,' Angry Dog replied (surprisingly, calmly, actually).

'Can you please just answer my question?'

'I said go away, you scrawny little mutt!'

At that, Rover wept and fled back to his kennel on the other side of the fence. *OK then,* he thought, *scrap the direct approach.* You see Rover was just trying to make Angry Dog feel better about himself, and he thought that the best way to start off was to find out what made him angry. A few minutes later, Rover was thinking about what could make Angry Dog so angry. Suddenly, he heard a purr and jumped right out of his kennel to see if there was a cat. 'Oh it's just you Danny, I thought you were one of those homeless cats from across the street,' he sighed.

'Yo! What's happenin' bro? I just saw what A D done to ya, so I'm gonna get over there and sort 'im out proper big time!' said Danny.

'You don't have to, Danny.'

'Yeah, well I'm gonna! He's always bossin' everyone about except for me! An' I ain't standin' for it no more!'

Just then it clicked for Rover. Angry Dog was scared of Danny! He quickly rushed over to the homeless cats in the street so that they could see him. The army of cats extracted their claws and showed their fangs. Rover ran for dear life. The lightning-fast cats sped after him in a tidal wave of fur and teeth.

Meanwhile, back at Angry Dog's house, Danny was aiming his pounce at Angry Dog, and checking the wind with his paw.

'Who's there?' yelled Angry Dog. Then he saw it, the tidal wave of cats. He stood up, took a deep breath, and let out the loudest, meanest, angriest bark he could! Rover heard it and stopped. The cats heard it and ran away in the other direction but, most importantly, Danny heard it, and sprinted back to his home!

The next day, Angry Dog was sitting, feeling awfully good after being told he'd scared Danny away and from that day on Angry Dog wasn't so angry anymore.

Phillip King (13)
Granville Community School, Swadlincote

Death Day

A boy not less than fourteen years old was stuck in his room, with his head against the misted cold window. It was Hallowe'en and he stared through the window, jealous of those who were out there. He wasn't allowed out, because he'd argued with his mum earlier over getting dirt on the new carpet, after playing football in the park.

Staring out of the window, whilst muttering angry thoughts, he didn't realise what he was looking at. It took him a few minutes before he noticed. A tall, dark, hooded figure around seven-foot in a large cloak, was walking down the street with what it looked like to be a long sharp axe in his hands. He fell back onto the floor out of shock, his head and back throbbing with pain. He got up, thinking, *that didn't look normal.*

A second glance out of the window showed him the figure walking towards the front door. What if it entered the house? Shaking with fear, he ran towards the airing cupboard, searching for his baseball bat, which he just couldn't find.

Just then, he heard the front door creak open. Peering down the stairs, he saw the tall figure entering. Paralysed with shock, he saw it gently close the door, and automatically look at him. It was a plain black shadow where the face should have been. But then, in one quick motion, it appeared in front of him, swished its axe as the boy's head fell to the floor.

Daniel Ellis (13)
Granville Community School, Swadlincote

The Prince And The Servant Girl

Once upon a time there was a tall dark prince and his controlling parents wanted him to have an arranged wedding with a dopey Spanish princess. But the prince was in love with the servant girl, and she was in love with him.

So late at night when the moon was shining bright they ran off together into the huge and dark woods (but they had each other, so that's all that mattered).

But this adventure is jam-packed with unfortunate events, so I will only mention a few. Firstly, a hungry pack of wolves, but the prince was quite a swordsman, so they escaped safely. Then they nearly fell into a quicksand pit.

But they found a vine-covered tiny cottage with a little red wooden door. It was perfect for them so they decided to live there so his parents couldn't find him. As all fairy stories end they lived happily ever after.

Katie Griffiths (13)
Granville Community School, Swadlincote

A Perfect Life

I will tell a tale of a famous girl called Sophia. Although she was invited to all the best parties, she was very sad. All her life she wished that she could have a normal life like all the other girls she met. She asked her mum and dad what she could do to make her happy? But they just told her to ride her horse.

When she turned sixteen, her life was still miserable, and had been for the past few years. While on the red carpet she saw the most handsome man in the world standing smiling to the crowd. She fell in love instantly and went to talk to him.

'Hi.'

They both started laughing. They got on well and she invited him over to her house later, he agreed. He was tall, dark and handsome with bright blue eyes and he was sixteen too!

As Sophia waited thinking he wasn't coming, there was a knock on the door and there he was. His name was Matt by the way. He stayed over that night and soon he proposed, and of course she said yes (by this time they were over twenty).

Not long after the marriage she sat him down and told him what a terrible life she'd had, although she'd had whatever she had wanted, a part of her life was missing, and that was a simple life!

So the story ends with Sophia ditching the glamour for her perfect life, and her own happiness.

Natasha Joseph (13)
Granville Community School, Swadlincote

The Vampires

One hundred years ago today, in a small house in a small village there lived a family. Susan, Dave and their children, Michael and Lucy. They were a normal family really, they did normal things and everyone knew them but no one really knew what they did.

Every night about 6pm after the sun had gone down, the family went out for their healthy walk. They did this every day. People saw them but they never saw them come back. Once they were out of sight, they would transform into bats because they were vampires!

Everything was going well as well as they could be, but all of a sudden people started going missing, but they weren't they were turning into bats. Susan and Dave had an idea to make everyone into bats so they wouldn't have to be so careful anymore. Every night they took one by one and eventually it worked, but they had nothing else to live off, but have they gone … ?

Holly Banton (12)
Granville Community School, Swadlincote

Memories

Once upon a time in a remote village called Turpentym, a young girl was lonely. Her mother had died and her father couldn't cope, so she lived with her grandma. Her grandma was rich and lived in the countryside far away from her father. The house was big and beautiful, but that was not what she wanted; she wanted her parents. Her parents' smell and warmth.

One night she was crying when she heard a sound. She went to her balcony door and standing there was the image of her mother. She turned her back as she was confused and scared, but her words were calming and reassuring. So she went to her mother. Her mum told her, 'I am going to take you on a journey that will make you laugh, cry and make you happy.'

Lucy was amazed and a little tired, so she went with her mother. She went back to all the awful memories and changed them. It was such an experience that when it came to saying goodbye, Lucy didn't want her to go. She knew she had to, but this was not what she wanted.

'Goodbye Lucy,' her mother calmly said.

'No ... Don't go ... pl- ...' Lucy's words trailed, as her mother grew wings and flew away.

Hannya Brown (13)
Granville Community School, Swadlincote

The Strange Adventure!

A long time ago there was a beautiful village where many happy families lived. There was one particular family; they were your average family. The eldest boy was thirteen, very daring and loved adventures, so when someone asked him if he wanted to see something special, he, of course, said yes!

He was led by the masked old woman through the village, through the wicked woods and then through a dark, spooky tunnel! As they walked through the endless tube the boy wondered if he had done the right thing. But after half an hour of walking in darkness, it came to an end. She then led him past a spooky-looking house.

Suddenly the old lady stopped abruptly at a small door, and rummaged around in her pocket, she then pulled out a large, oddly-shaped key! As soon as she had unlocked the door she gestured him in, and cold, damp air hit him sharply. He was now wishing he had never come.

After walking through another cold, dark tunnel, the woman stopped and looked at the boy. She then pulled out a piece of paper from her bottomless pocket, it was an agreement! It stated that the boy could come here whenever he wanted and even bring a friend, but he could not tell an adult or something bad might happen. The woman then held a pen out to the boy and he signed it, not really knowing what he was about to see. He followed the woman and there, before his eyes, was a magnificent funfair, with rides and candyfloss - anything you could think of.

The woman said, 'This is all yours!' and left.

Laura Fearn (13)
Granville Community School, Swadlincote

What Would You Do?

'What would you do?' Megan laughed as she spoke to Emma. 'And then,' she said, 'he tripped and spilt the Coke all down Emily! I couldn't stop laughing!'

Emma laughed as well. They were walking along the road on a hot, summer's afternoon. 'Talking of Coke, I'm really thirsty,' said Emma, 'where shall we go?'

'Let's go to McDonald's, we can get food then as well.'

'Alright then, let's go there.'

As they walked, a man covered in something red ran past them. They thought nothing of it and carried on. When they turned down an alleyway they saw someone against the wall.

'I wonder who it is?' said Megan.

'Listen, they're crying, Meg. What shall we do?'

They walked over to where the person sat.

'Oh my God! It's Emily!' whispered Emma.

'You can an ambulance while I sort her out,' said Meg.

Suddenly Emily lifted her head and moaned. 'Meg? Emma? Is that you?' moaned Emily. 'Help please!'

'Emily, what's happened?' asked Megan.

'Some bloke jumped on me and and - ' moaned Emily.

'Did he hurt you, Em?'

'Yes, he, he -' Emily burst into tears.

'OK, Emily, the ambulance will be here soon,' Emma told her.

Megan and Emma hugged Emily and kept her warm until the ambulance came. When it arrived, Emma and Megan helped Emily onto the ambulance and stayed with her.

The man they saw was arrested and is now serving ten years in prison. Sadly Emily died four hours after Megan and Emma found her because of twelve stab wounds.

Megan and Emma were rewarded for helping Emily.

Lauren Griffiths (13)
Granville Community School, Swadlincote

Football Fantastico!

Wednesday 10th May. A beautiful sun was shining and there wasn't a cloud in the sky today. It's the Champions League Final. Arsenal v Barcelona in Paris, France. Both teams have put out their best sides. Arsenal with Henry on top form, also Francesc Fabregas, Sol Campbell and Cole back from injury. Arsenal have a great chance of lifting the trophy, but I wouldn't count Barcelona out. They have the legendary goofy-teethed Ronaldinho and Eto'o who are on top form.

This shapes up to be a great final. The whistle blows, we're off. Arsenal pass from right to left and are settling into a possession game. A slip from Toure lets Ronaldinho clean through. Lehmann comes out and Ronaldinho back heels it to the running Eto'o who places the ball into the back of the net.

1-0 Barcelona.

From then on Barcelona take it to Arsenal for the rest of the half, but Arsenal hold out.

Half-time.

Arsenal come out all guns blazing and Henry bends a 30-yard screamer past Valdes into the top corner.

Arsenal 1-1 Barcelona.

The score stays the same till penalties.

0 = goal
X = miss
Penalties
Henry 0
Ljungberg 0
Pires X
Reyes 0
Fabregas 0
Ronaldinho 0
Deco 0
Messi X
Larsson 0
Eto'o X
Arsenal win. Yes!

Peter Wright (13)
Granville Community School, Swadlincote

The Break-In

Jamie and I sat in my bedroom with a layout of old Mr Smith's house stuck on the wall. It was going to be an easy job. Mr Smith was loaded, pensioners always are, money lying everywhere waiting for robbers to break in and steal it.

It was midnight and Mr Smith had just turned his light off and stumbled into bed. Time for action. We stuck on our black balaclavas and jumpers and sprinted down the stairs. We picked up our BB guns off the kitchen table and quietly stepped out the front door.

The night was warm and the moon was bright. We walked through the garden and then leapt over the garden fence. Mr Smith's back door was locked tight but we often saw him put a spare key in the plant pot next to the door. I picked it up and slowly slid it into the lock. *Click.* The door was open. I entered with Jamie following slowly behind.

I was cold and scared but determined. I entered the room slowly and looked around for something that an old man might hide money in. Then in the corner of my eye I saw a large silver safe. I tiptoed over to it and carefully moved the lock around. Suddenly a loud alarm sounded and a police car parked outside the house. I'd forgotten the police station was only down the road. An officer bashed down the front door and ran into the room where we were. He pulled out a gun and aimed it at me. I stood shaking when the BB gun fell out of my pocket. The officer looked scared.

That was when the first shot was fired.

Andrew Billings (13)
Granville Community School, Swadlincote

Get Out!

'Hiya Chloe, where are we going today?'

'Shall we go check out that haunted house?'

'OK then.'

'See ya Yazza.'

'See ya.'

Yazza was walking to Chloe's house when she got a text from Chloe saying that she wasn't at home but at the haunted house.

So Yazza turned back and walked through the black gates that were as tall as skyscrapers. The squeak shivered down her spine.

Chloe shouted, 'I'm over here!'

Chloe and Yazza walked through the doors of the house.

'Did you hear that Yazza?'

Yazza shook her head.

Chloe told Yazza it was the first room they were going in. Yazza wasn't keen, but they went in.

'Get out!' a voice shouted.

Yazza ran straight out of the house.

Chloe heard laughing. *That sounds like Josh,* she thought to herself. She stood there thinking then she got out her phone and rang Josh.

She heard his phone ringing. Josh came down and muttered, 'Why do girls always trick us?'

'You're the one who needs to get out!' shouted Chloe as she pushed him out of the door!

Amy Beaman (12)
Granville Community School, Swadlincote

The Girl Who Disappeared?

In a faraway village called Melbow, there was a school. The school was at night. The school was as black as a rubber tyre. There was something strange about this particular school. But what? The spooky school was as cold as a polar bear. Mist was beginning to circulate around the school.

One afternoon a girl called Hannah, who is 13 and a very bright student, was walking towards her classroom when she walked past the headteacher's office where she saw an unusual shapeless figure. So she decided to go and check it out after her class. The bell rang so she ran as fast as she could to the headteacher's.

When everyone had left except her she quietly opened the door, the door slammed, *bang!* and the headteacher grabbed her, and no one has ever seen or heard what has happened to her since.

The only thing left of her is in the headteacher's office. A tiny, little, little, little voice saying, 'Help me, help me, please help me.'

Some people say she is dead, something says she was murdered, some say she ran away, and some people say she disappeared, but no one knows where she is.

Is she alive or is she dead?

Lauren Bailey (12)
Humphrey Perkins High School & Community Centre, Loughborough

The Vicar's Death

It was a cold, dark, misty night at the local church ten years ago. The vicar was sorting out papers, as he sat in his ornate wooden chair. Someone knocked on the door. An owl hooted in the background. The door slowly creaked open. The misty, black figure was a huge giant with enormous feet that clonked to the floor.

The dark, mysterious figure moved closer towards the vicar. He stood up out of his chair, putting his hands on the desk in front of him. 'What can I do for you?' asked the vicar. There was no reply. *Bang!* The vicar screamed intensely and then dropped to the floor, dead. Someone had shot him.

A new vicar took his place. Three days later he was at the altar praying. The church door slammed open and a pale-looking figure lurched forwards. Black, the vicar, ran out of the back door.

'You cannot run, I will always find you!' the dead man said.

Black ran outside. Hands began to come out of the ground. All the dead surrounded him.

'You took my life. Now I will take yours, Victor Black!' All the dead crookedly walked forwards.

'Argh!' Victor screamed and then lay dead on the lawn.

Victor Black had been murdered by the ghost who he had murdered. The dead vicar crawled inside Victor's body and walked back into the church. No one ever suspected a thing! as they thought they were being preached to by Black.

Bethany Kell (13)
Humphrey Perkins High School & Community Centre, Loughborough

Disappeared

It was a cold, windy night and nothing could be seen because of the mist. Their breath was cold as it came out of their mouths. They could feel their hairs on their arms sticking up! When they walked they hadn't a clue where they were going. As they crept out of the house they looked behind them, they could see nothing, it was like they were going blind, and all they could see was grey! They heard something! Something rustle! It was just dried leaves blowing around in the wind. The family lived in the middle of nowhere. The village was miles away!

Living in the house was a dad (Alan), a girl (Jasmine) and a dog (Oscar). Jasmine was 13 years old and was clever for her age!

All of them were in the lounge watching TV, then they heard a noise. It sounded like footprints. It was as loud as an elephant! They all went upstairs to investigate! Jas got scared standing on the landing and saw … no one. But still heard footprints. Alan disappeared!

Jas was scared as a mouse. She heard her dad's voice. Then she screamed! Jas saw her dad. As she went to hug him, she fell straight through him. He was now a ghost! Jas heard a scream. Oscar went mad and ran to the wardrobe. There she found her mum and brother Tom.

Alan stayed as a ghost but stayed with them. They were as happy as a summer's day!

Lydia Hall (12)
Humphrey Perkins High School & Community Centre, Loughborough

Who's There?

The boarding school was old, dark and gloomy where the walls and floor were damp with rainwater from the hole in the roof. The carpet was coming up and most of the windows smashed. All you could hear were floorboards creaking and wind whistling throughout the entire house. In the middle of nowhere with miles upon miles of creepy, misty wood there was no one to see and nowhere to go.

She had no idea why her father, an ordinary man with brown shabby hair and scruffy clothes, wanted to buy this forgotten place, it was a challenge they would never forget. She was eight at the time. She walked into the house and took a glance around. She shuddered at the thought that she might have to live in this house of which was rotten, wet and smelly.

The day after they had arrived, her dad started to fix the roof. She lay on the bed and looked up at the ceiling. She heard someone, she ran into all of the rooms and there was no one around, yet she could still hear the voice. Then it shouted her name. She walked around the corner, looking in every direction, her heart thumping, then suddenly something grabbed her from behind and started laughing as it pulled her down to the cellar. She shouted to her dad but he couldn't hear her. There was nothing she could do, it had got her forever.

Jade Kunne (13)
Humphrey Perkins High School & Community Centre, Loughborough

The Lonely Lake

'Help me Mummy, help me!'

Six years later …

On the edge of a long-lost village at the end of a winding road stood an old stone building. The mansion emerged through thick, frosty clouds of mist. It creaked with age as the whistling wind whirled around the building. Six-year-old Molly left her mansion to visit the lake at the bottom of her never-ending garden. As she fought her way down, withered branches reached to grab her. Beneath Molly's feet the grass crunched like ice.

Suddenly Molly felt a shiver down her spine, she heard a rustle, a boy appeared from nowhere. 'What are you doing here?' Molly asked, shivering in shock.

'My name is Ben, I used to live here.' He glided onto the middle of the lake. Molly was speechless. 'You should see the bottom. I first saw it when I died. I was vigorously pushed by this woman, I drowned instantly.'

Over dinner, Molly told her mum about Ben, and how he walked on water.

'Really, darling, don't start imagining things again, it'll give you nightmares,' Molly's mum explained doubtfully.

Splash! Molly had attempted to walk on water.

As it grew darker Molly's mum called her. 'Ben, there's my mum,' Molly murmured as they went onto the middle of the lake. Horrified and shocked her mum screamed.

'That's the woman who killed me!' Ben started crying.

'But …' Molly sobbed.

Ben turned away.

'She is my mum.'

Joanne Paul (13)
Humphrey Perkins High School & Community Centre, Loughborough

Madness!

The lost, dark house was lonely and plain, the doors creaked as the wind blew through the windows, and the old woman sat, sobbing in her sleep.

Her husband was dead, he took his own life, she had been filled with grief ever since. As she sat, still asleep, she was awoken by a deafening scream. Her nerves were on edge and the slightest thing would upset her. Scared but curious about the noise she went to see what it was. Moving down the three levels of the house, she passed big paintings, cobwebs, and as she walked, she felt more and more like she was being followed, all the time being drawn towards the cellar door.

As she slowly opened the door, she felt a sudden rush of fear. As she moved, cobwebs and dust flew into her face and a sickening smell got stronger with every step she took. It'd been a long time since she'd been down here, but she still knew where things were. As she looked into the corner, she saw a shape that wasn't familiar. As she stepped towards it, the smell got stronger. She slowly leant forward to touch it and felt the fabric of a blanket. She slowly uncovered the object to a smell that was unbearable. At that moment she realised that she was standing over her husband's dead body. She turned to run, screaming uncontrollably. She stopped suddenly, looking out of the window. An unnatural calmness flowed through her as she launched herself out of the window.

Jessica Ball (13)
Humphrey Perkins High School & Community Centre, Loughborough

The Lost Island

It was just getting dark and the mist was getting thicker, bats were circling around the lost bay and the sea was so calm, it was spooky. The only sound that could be heard was the gentle waves moving slowly inwards. There was a full moon in the sky, and it was imposing, scary and haunting, it could only just be made out through the layer of mist acting as a wall, limiting sight and in the middle of all this there was a boy.

This boy's name was Jake, he had been shipwrecked on this island, everyone else was lost and he had been washed ashore. Jake was 13 years old and had short brown hair. He was in good physical shape and was very strong. As he looked around he saw he was on a beach, with only one way to go, inland.

Half an hour later, Jake finally got to a pair of gates towering over him like two giants and engraved at the top in dark, gloomy letters was 'The Manor'. As he pushed open the gates a creaking noise cut through the air. Jake walked up to the house that was part hidden in mist and undergrowth. The garden was overgrown and shadows lurked behind every bush. The Manor was ghostly and was covered in vines and cobwebs. The windows were smashed in and there was only one light coming from the top bedroom. It was his only hope, this house. So Jake pulled the doorbell chain, the sound vibrated into the night. Then the door opened ...

James Myers (13)
Humphrey Perkins High School & Community Centre, Loughborough

Redex Valley!

In Redex Valley was a night unlike any other. It was a foggy yet misty day, but by night, the sky became eerie, empty, a ghost town. No one went out and no one opened their shops - there was something about that night. The atmosphere was cold and as black as a black cat's eyes.

That night all started when Jocko' Rope moved into Redex. Many had seen him before wandering the graveyards, but it may have been the fog playing tricks on them. One thing about Jocko was that he never left his property, and he always wore a suit with no tie.

One night Salty Salta' - boy was messing around and he decided to go into Jocko's house.

'Hey! What are you doing in here?' the large man shouted.

'Erm … I …' the boy was shaking now as he was in the man's room, it was full of hanging ropes, and ties hanging from the ceiling.

'Now you know how I died, and why I never wear ties - because it traps my throat as I've been hung seven times!' The man said in a deep voice, now walking to the boy with a rope in his hand.

'No please … wait!' and that was the last anyone ever heard of little boy, Salty Salta'!

After that, no one lived in Redex, but it wasn't called Redex anymore, it was called Dead-X! Named after Jocko' Rope!

Amy Hunter (12)
Humphrey Perkins High School & Community Centre, Loughborough

The Attic

It was a cold, dark winter's night. All of the family were sitting by the fire. The room was dark and lit only by the fire. Sally and Ric went to their room. They settled down in bed. Suddenly they heard a noise coming from the attic.

Sally was eight-years-old. She had long brown hair and brown eyes. Ric was 12, he also had brown hair and brown eyes.

'Ric, what was that?' Sally shivered.

'I'm not sure but I'm going to find out.' Ric got out of bed and stood on the landing with Sally behind. Suddenly there was another noise. Ric didn't flinch he just reached out and got the ladder. Suddenly out of nowhere, the ladder fell down and a voice said, 'Go back, this house is haunted.'

'That sounded like Grandma,' said Sally.

'But it can't be, she's downstairs,' Ric explained.

Another voice spoke, 'No, no, come up.' The voice was calm and hypnotising and made both Sally and Ric want to climb back up to the attic. They got up there and found a picture of a woman from the past. Suddenly the picture was ripped off them. Against their judgement they followed it as it went into a corner where they saw their nanny.

'Argh!' both children screamed.

'Don't scream,' hushed a voice coming from their nanny's mouth, but wasn't their nanny's voice. The children screamed and headed for the ladder. As Sally put her foot on the ladder she heard her nanny's voice, 'No, don't leave me,' she cried.

Sally left the ladder and headed for her nanny She grabbed her arm and powerfully pulled her down. There was a thud, then both Sally and her nanny got up. Ric stared in amazement.

'What was that noise?' asked their mother.

'I'm not sure,' Nanny Beckles said as if she didn't know.

''We're not sure,' said Sally and Ric shakily.

'Well, night then.'

Abigail Bates (13)
Humphrey Perkins High School & Community Centre, Loughborough

Ghost Story

It was midnight and homeless James and John were round the campfire in the woods. There were owls hooting and trees swishing and swaying in the wind. James was just about to doze off when all of a sudden the campfire went out. James looked up and there were no ashes. James jumped up and woke John, they both ran until they got tired, then they thought they would stop in a hedge to sleep.

Next morning they both woke up and looked in front of them, and saw this old rusty 4x4 landrover. They looked at each other, jumped up and looked inside. The keys were in but it wouldn't start, it was obvious that it had been here for quite a while. They tried as hard as they could to get it going but it wouldn't start. James said that they could both sleep in it tonight, so they did.

When they woke up they opened their eyes and found they were the middle of a town. They opened the bonnet and there was no engine. John pushed it off the road, got back in and all of a sudden heard an engine noise; he looked behind and in front, but could not see any cars. All of a sudden they jolted forward at a frightening speed. James and John both fainted, and woke up in a car crash. They were both rushed to a nearby hospital but later died.

Matthew Mills (12)
Humphrey Perkins High School & Community Centre, Loughborough

Untitled

I'm here, staring into the future, with hardly any past behind me. I see great nature working against my plan.

The uncontrolled waves smack and shatter against the rocks as I slowly start forcing the small boat out on the sea.

It's fairly warm, but my own lips seem to tremble, as they touch the mist of the salty water. As I crawl into the boat, I suddenly feel great pain in my lower part of my right leg. I look with pain and see a lazily sticking-out nail which has ripped out a chunk of flesh. But being behind the waves, which stop getting trespassers through, there is no sense to go back. No one would help me anyway.

Feeling sick, I still put up the sail. I lay on the boat, looking at the sky, as my eyes are opened up with pure sunlight. I close my eyes.

I wake up, still keeping my eyes closed. This time, my whole body complete with pain, like I'm being shot with a continuous machine gun with no feelings. As I open up my tired red eyes, I see rain falling down on us; the sea, boat and I.

I sit up, look around and still feel my wound. I quickly look at it finding myself laying in a puddle of blood. I stand up with great difficulty, putting all my weight on my left leg and pulling myself up by the sail.

I jump. As I hit the surface of the sea, I feel my body refreshing. Once again I open up my eyes and feel the contact with the water.

Stupidity is faced and the predator comes.

Richard Pniewski (14)
Trinity Catholic High School, Woodford Green

Caught In The Moment

The same thing happens every day, nothing different ever happens. All the time, all I do is wake up and go to school.

Katie strolled downstairs and started packing her school bag. Katie shouted out to her mum, 'I'm going now, bye,' and she left the house, slamming the door behind her. Katie then saw her boyfriend, Scott, across the road where he waited for her every morning. She called across to him and, without looking, ran straight across the road. She looked up at Scott and his eyes started to fill with tears. Katie couldn't understand why he was crying.

The next morning she woke up and went downstairs, again the same thing was happening. She walked outside to meet Scott but he wasn't there. Then she remembered him crying yesterday and thought maybe it was for the same reason.

She walked down her path and there at the end was a large bunch of flowers. Katie didn't understand why, and just laughed. Inside the flowers was a small note, that said, 'Katie, I love you and will miss you always, RIP love Scott!'

Then it all came flashing back. Running in the road, the blue Mercedes and the ambulance. Katie wasn't laughing anymore.

Claire Mulvey (15)
Trinity Catholic High School, Woodford Green

A Day In The Life Of A Soldier

I couldn't bear to think about the day ahead. I was so scared. Nerves ran through me like water from a tap as it approached noon. I had to stay strong for Bob. He looked up to me, poor lad, thought I wasn't afraid of anything. He couldn't be more wrong, but I couldn't let him see that.

As we changed into our camouflage suits, our marshal gave us our orders and told us where to go on the battlefield. He told me and Bob to prepare and go and load our guns, and for Bob to get the team flag. I turned to him with a brave stern voice and said, 'You can do it Bob, be brave.' He replied with a nod.

Ready, steady, go! That's it, no turning back now. The guns were spitting out bullets, men were going down. I had to be brave, swallow my pride, do it for my team. I looked at Bob, signalling that I would cover his back as he made a run for it with the flag. *Splat!* A bullet hit Bob right between the eyes. My heart raced as he was dragged off the battlefield. I was the only man from my team left. That was it, I made a run for it and as I decided to throw the flag into the opposition's castle, I got hit. It landed on target. We celebrated to our victory of the blue team. What a wicked day of paintballing.

Alisha Cullen (15)
Trinity Catholic High School, Woodford Green

A Day In The Life Of White Hart Lane

It was the big day, Saturday, the match day, every football fan's favourite day. It was Tottenham versus Arsenal, my favourite day. It is eagerly anticipated by every fan. The only problem is the fans can get a little over excited.

It was nearing 12 o'clock and the staff and officials were starting to turn up to the ground. I was even getting nervous, well I do get to see every match for free. The officials were coming out to check to see if the pitch was in good condition and then they went back in.

The next thing I heard was a coach pull up, it must have been the players. I was so excited, because then I knew it was getting closer and closer to 3 o'clock. The fans were pouring in from all corners of the ground. A massive cheer went up as the players came out. It was time. The football was end to end but was spoilt by a couple of hundred fans who started a fight, which turned into a disaster for me. I knew my time was coming to an end. I was hoping the stewards would calm them down before I would crack.

Everyone rushed out of me like I was going to crumble. To the liking of the Arsenal fans I did it. Looking at the faces of the Tottenham fans they weren't happy because they had lost their stadium and would have to fork out money to put me right again.

Daniel Meader (15)
Trinity Catholic High School, Woodford Green

World War III

The Germans had once again taken over Europe but nobody would have thought that England was stopping them from doing so once again. Frank was an RAF pilot and had been for the last six years. He had always trained for combat but had never thought there would be another war in the year 2005.

Frank and his two friends, Mark and Scott, were told urgently to get into the air because the Germans had dropped two bombs on Southampton's port.

The bullets and missiles had started flying around the Southampton sky. Frank was keeping in contact with his two friends when suddenly Mark began shouting faster, nervously. It was because he had been hit and the roof of his plane was jammed. The signal between them then cut off. Frank looked over his shoulder to see a RAF plane burning inches from the ground.

A German plane had come into sight and in anger Frank flew after it, not looking behind him.

Scott shouted, 'Get out of there, Frank,' but he only had one thing on his mind, so ignored him and launched two missiles at the plane that had shot down his friend. Frank had taken his mind off of the 'dog fight' taking place around him in the air only to look to his left and see a missile heading for him, he stopped instantly, his eyes focused on the missile heading straight for him.

Lewis Board (15)
Trinity Catholic High School, Woodford Green

Attack

As dusk approached, I was landing in America, so I was going to be resting in Chicago for the night. It was around two in the morning when I woke. I had heard shuffling in and weird noises from the rear end of where I was staying that night. I also heard talking; but not English, a language that I had never heard before, which is unusual for my line of work. I would have gone and checked it out, but I had work in the morning, so I decided to leave it and get my sleep.

I awoke to a sunny American day. I was expecting my usual workers today, but for a strange reason I had different workers. These workers didn't speak English either, they spoke a foreign language, a language again that I had never heard before. I thought that it was a bit peculiar, but as normal I began work. Everything began as normal. I noticed there was a problem when I heard an unperformed speech from the captain. The speech followed by screams and gunshots. The captain then began to lose control of the plane. The plane then began to drop lower and lower. I heard more screams and more gunshots. The plane dropped lower still. More screams and gunshots. Until a ear-shattering noise came upon us.

That was when I realised, I had just crashed into the North World Trade Centre Tower.

Charlie Bostock (15)
Trinity Catholic High School, Woodford Green

Mortifying Mansion

Harry, smile on face and book in hand, strolled down the long narrow street after the end of the school term. He passed the old Whitman place as usual except today the windows were unboarded.

To Harry this made no sense, that house he knew had been abandoned for 50 years. The history of the place was legendary. Mr Whitman and his family were said to be buried in the house. Everyone in the whole of Sunshine Meadow avoided the house like the plague. People would cross the road, even if they were going out of their way just to avoid this house.

However, Harry all the same needed to know more about the place and why people were so scared of it. Harry's curiosity burning inside, had to wait, until night-time also he knew to bring someone along with him. Andy, his best friend perhaps.

They both ran from their comfy homes to the Whitman place. Gently pushing open the door, they noticed gigantic suits of armour. A distant crashing and clanging aroused their curiosity. The sight of another human being gave them a start.

Four people sat at the table. They were the Whitmans, they had pretended to the public they were dead and the house was possessed to stop it from being smashed down and become flats. No one dared go in and check because they feared they would meet the same fate as the Whitmans. Harry and Andy forgot they still had one more big problem … *their parents!*

Channing Gardner (12)
Trinity Catholic High School, Woodford Green

Not One Murder But Two

'What are you doing?' Mrs Redrum shouted, as her son walked on her beige carpet. She left a bright red mark on his forehead before he passed out and fell to the ground.

She looked at him and to her horror he was dead! She pulled him into the front garden and threw him on the pavement, then she phoned the police and said that she had found her son dead on the pavement outside her house.

The police arrived within minutes of her calling them, then they looked at each other and murmured a few things, and told her it was not a job for them, but a job for detective Bill.

Detective Bill started to examine the body straight away, and tried to work out who could have killed the boy. He went through the list of all the murderers and realised that the way the boy was killed was like no other and the only suspects were three villagers. The detective slowly cancelled out each of the suspects by evidence and got his final suspect.

He told her what he had discovered while she rolled her eyes with anger and disbelief, and after he had finished, she jumped straight at him, and pushed him to the ground …

Charlotte Carnell (12)
Trinity Catholic High School, Woodford Green

A Visit To Her Grave

'Honey, honey, wake up! It's time …'

As Lorraine Turner burst into tears, Lorraine's husband, Drake, didn't say a word, just stood in one position. He didn't even have the strength to blink. Ten minutes had passed, only then did they get dressed. Lorraine had dressed in all black.

As she entered the kitchen, Drake had already got dressed in a black suit which was as dark as a blink. He was preparing the flowers.

'I'll take those from you.' Lorraine whispered, as she made a bouquet.

Along the driveway to the graveyard, a black Hearse pulled up by an empty hole in the cemetery. Above the hole was a gravestone. It read: 'In loving memory of our daughter, Tilly Turner who died on …'

They planted their flowers and said goodbye. It was time to go.

That night they both had a dream. A horrific dream.

In the morning they told each other their dream. Funny, they were the same. Later that day, they were preparing flowers yet again.

At seven o'clock they went to visit their daughter's grave. No moonlight but there was howling. Lorraine and Drake stepped up to Tilly's grave - they spoke to her. Then screeching screams from her parents occurred. They were sucked into her grave by her hands.

It had been days since they'd been seen. Only the detectives could find them.

When they looked into their bedroom, they saw blood slowly appearing on their bed. Then their flesh and bones … but there was nothing that could be done.

Vivien Bodnar (12)
Trinity Catholic High School, Woodford Green

The Amazing Adventure Of The Bank Robbers

Andrew and Ethan's parents were in huge debt. So they decided to do something about it.

'Look at all the security cameras, we'll never get past them!' cried Ethan, as he and his brother stood outside the estate's biggest bank.

'You're a computer genius, you'll find a way to switch them off,' said Andrew.

That night, using the home computer, Ethan hacked into the bank's security system. Meanwhile, Andrew anxiously packed the backpacks with: ropes, gloves, torches, a large holdall to carry the cash and one firework.

Both boys, dressed in black, set off into the night.

'OK, this is what we do,' ordered Andrew. 'I'll go round the back and you follow!'

Andrew, using the ropes, was the first to walk up the wall and onto the glass dome roof. Once there, he pulled Ethan up.

'Just crack the glass and I'll climb down,' said Ethan.

Once in, they walked down to the vault.

'We've only got one firework so we better pray this works!' cried Andrew.

Boom!

Whaw-whaw-whaw-whaw.

'The police!' screamed Ethan.

As the sound of footsteps approached the boys quickly climbed into the vents. The door opened; through the gaps in the vent the boys could see the top of the officers' heads.

'They're gonna find us!' shouted Ethan.

'What was that?' asked Parker.

'Probably someone outside,'

'What about the vents?'

'No, only a child would be able to fit in there!' said Officer Chris Parker.

'I still managed to fill the bag,' giggled Andrew. 'Now let's get out of here!'

Kate Underwood (12)
Trinity Catholic High School, Woodford Green

Murder From The Past

I felt a painful breeze slither down my spine! I peered at what was ahead of me! Metal gates revealed a haunted building ... I tore the icy gates apart, and stumbled up a stone path. Soon I got to a door. As I took my first step into the building I heard a high-pitched scream! The door behind me slammed!

Peering ahead worriedly, my heart froze as I saw prison cells. It felt like someone had shot me in my ears when I heard voices screaming at me! I walked on, my hands clasped to my ears, the noise was unbearable. Hands were reaching out grabbing me! There was no flesh on their bodies. They were skeletons!

Terrified, I sprinted down the corridor, it didn't seem to end. The skeletons were sliding through the bars! A window was ahead. I realised that the only way out was to jump through the window! As the window was coming closer to me, I leapt!

I woke up to find myself in a deserted barber shop. A pale lady yelled, 'Sweeney Todd victi-err, customer!'

A man wearing a spotless apron glided into the room! The lady shoved me onto a chair. Sweeney Todd got a pair of scissors, and slowly trimmed my hair, with a sudden movement he grabbed a knife, and I felt a sharp sudden pain rush across my throat.

Everything went black! I began to see pictures of famous murderers appearing in my head. I saw Sweeney Todd, Jack the Ripper and more!

Rosie Bostock (12)
Trinity Catholic High School, Woodford Green

The Christmas Mystery

On Christmas Day, Mark, Sam and Lizzy were taking turns to open presents. Mark eagerly ripped the glistening paper off a long package, which he was hoping would be a keyboard, but it turned out to be a paper trimmer. He sighed in disappointment.

Later on, all of the presents had been opened, except one. They all stared at it in silence.

'Why don't we open it together?' Sam suggested.

Without a sound, they slowly tore open the crumpled paper. It was a small box of 'Fizzmelt' chocolates.

'Hey, I've heard of these, they're supposed to fizz as the chocolate melts,' Lizzy whispered. Soon, they all began to tuck into the chocolates.

Meanwhile, the rest of the neighbourhood were at the police station collecting their presents which had apparently been stolen.

Mr Baker and his two children, William and Danny, were asked a few routine questions by Inspector Bailey.

'So, did you catch the thieves?' asked William curiously.

'Well,' replied Inspector Bailey, 'they gave themselves in, after eating poisoned 'Fizzmelt' chocolates. However, we could not question them as they died soon after.'

'How tragic!' Danny said, sniggering.

'Anyway, we have now found the culprit who murdered the thieves. Danny, you are under arrest!'

Danny was taken away without another word.

'The chocolates were meant to be for *you*, Mr Baker; Danny wanted to murder *you* so he could run away and take your money!' Inspector Bailey stated. William and Mr Baker stared in amazement.

The rest of Christmas Day was spent in shock and disbelief. This was the worst Christmas the Baker family had ever had.

Rebecca Andrews (12)
Trinity Catholic High School, Woodford Green

One More Night

Her feet pounded down on the concrete floor, her heart was pumping in her ears. Her lungs were screaming for air but she refused to stop, she had to keep running. Her shadow cast a gangly figure across the pavement, as she took her fleeting steps forward.

The moonlight was reflected in a puddle beneath her but she failed to stop. She fell to the floor with a loud crack. Gritting her teeth with pain, she rolled onto her side and spat out the thick dark blood clogging her throat. As she stood she saw her pale reflection in a window. Her black hair matted to her forehead, blood dripping down her chin. She looked awful but she needed to tell someone.

She reached her door and fumbled for her keys. The door finally burst open to reveal her room mate Karen cooking over the stove.

'I saw him,' the girl said quietly.

'Who?' Karen asked, her brow wrinkling.

The girl raised a quivering hand at the television screen. A police sketch showed a masked man, knife in hand and mangled body beneath him.

'Him!' Karen shouted, her face devastated. There was a sudden deafening bang. The girl lay slumped on the doorstep, dead.

Karen said nothing, but simply picked up the phone and dialled.

'You didn't have to kill her,' she said darkly.

'She saw me, I had to do something.'

'Don't make the same mistake again.'

Karen hung up and went back to her cooking. For one more night at least the Woodford Green serial killer was free.

Megan Gaffey (12)
Trinity Catholic High School, Woodford Green

I Remember

As I woke up I tried to sit, but my body ached. I rubbed my head and as I groggily looked around, realised everything was somehow different. As I stood up, I was confused to find I'd been sleeping right by the edge of a lake. This scared me a little as I could have easily just drowned. Why was I there?

I slowly began walking, although I was now unaware of where I was going. Blinding lights flashed in my eyes when I passed certain places, making me stop and grab my throbbing head. Images swam around me, as if they had actually happened. I heard someone scream and it all stopped.

I let go of my head and turned around. I was back at the lake, the exact spot where I'd woken. I was terrified. I knew I hadn't walked back this way, and was scared to find out how I'd managed to subconsciously return. What had happened here?

As I woke up I tried to sit, but my head ached. Finally I had remembered. There was no way I could ever escape this lake, unless my body was found. I'd spent ages trying to forget which is why it was so hard to remember.

Sydney Sims (15)
Trinity Catholic High School, Woodford Green

Untitled

First day of spring, trees blossom, birds sing and families sit in the garden. It was a perfect day and Grandma decided to sweep up the last of the autumn leaves while she could keep an eye on the children.

'Grandma!' they screamed excitedly as she entered the garden. 'Grandma, we're bored!'

'Why don't you go and explore?' she answered.

'No,' they replied, 'that's boring.'

'When I was your age I used to go on adventures with my sister and we found some amazing things,' Grandma told them.

'What did you find Grandma, please tell us?' they asked.

'Well there was this one time …

… I was about your age when we discovered it, it was amazing. I could hear it, I could feel it, I could even smell it.'

The children were confused, but listened as she carried on.

'We were searching the garden for something to do but we found nothing, so we sat on the grass to think, then I closed my eyes and thought the hardest I ever have. Then I saw it, my fantasy world, it was everything I had ever imagined; the sweet smell of candyfloss made my mouth water, the sound of the tigers and people's laughter and the surroundings were so energetic. I went there a lot in my childhood, I was able to go any time. I wanted to escape the world for just a few seconds.'

'Where did you go, Grandma, were you abducted by aliens? How can we go there?' they asked, not completely understanding.

Grandma replied, 'If you want to go to your fantasy world you have to use your imagination and let it guide you.'

Emma Cullen (14)
Trinity Catholic High School, Woodford Green

1999

Adam awoke gasping, fumbling to reach his ringing alarm clock from underneath the pile of books, underwear and rubbish. He glanced over at the computer screen, noting the countdown to the new millennium was fast approaching. Clambering over the mounds of clothing, he reached for the mouse. His computer burst to life as he tried to clear his files of the crippling virus that threatened the world's computer systems. A mysterious onlooker had sent the email to every account across the world, but the antidote to its effects had yet to be found. Scientists were desperately attempting to find a remedy for the deadly bug, but the security lock placed on its files had limited access to its data.

Adam opened his inbox, staring at the seemingly innocent email. Disguised as spam, many email users opened the file and released the devastation within. Once the virus was activated, it shut down the whole system, resulting in a total loss of information, on the strike of the new millennium. The bug could destroy data from organisations such as the FBI and MI5, causing mass panic. Adam turned on the radio, listening for Millennium Bug updates.

'We interrupt this broadcast to inform listeners of the development in the 'Millennium Bug' antidote.' Adam stared intently at the speakers, stunned. 'A code has been created that will utilise the problems created by the bug.' Adam was stunned, feeling relieved at the cure. He typed the numbers into his account: 8 16 27 36.

'Deactivating Virus.'

Emily Boulton (15)
Trinity Catholic High School, Woodford Green

Murder In The House

Karen was on her usual trip to work. She was walking fast because she was late.

'Argh!' She stumbled to the ground.

'Can I help you?' A gentleman insisted taking her hand.

'Sorry.'

'No worries, I'm Mark.'

'I'm Karen.' Silence struck as they were gazing into each other's eyes.

'Do you want a lift?' he kindly offered.

'If that's okay with you.'

'Yes sure.' They decided to have dinner together. They had only just met but Mark knew that she was 'the one'. At the restaurant Mark and Karen had such a fantastic time. Mark ordered some chocolate for Karen.

'Ow, what's this?' she chewed on something hard. It was a shiny diamond ring.

'Will you marry me Karen?'

'Yes I will marry you.'

Soon they got married and they were living together, but she didn't know his past - that he'd been sent to jail for murder. One day Karen started getting suspicious. So she called her dad to see if he could work out what he was hiding.

'Mark, my dad is coming over for dinner.'

'I will be glad to meet him.' A few minutes later her father came.

'Hi I'm Derek,' he introduced himself to Mark. 'Can I use your toilet?'

'Yes it's upstairs on the left.'

Derek went to the bedroom instead and he found all the newspapers of when he was a murderer.

Mark thought he was taking too long so he went to see if he was alright. Derek wasn't answering so he poked his head through but he wasn't there, so he rushed straight to his room, and Mark found him scurrying through his drawers.

'So now you know the truth, it's been nice knowing you.' Mark pulled out a penknife out of his pocket.

'Nooo!' but she was too late, her dad was found drenched in blood.

'You killed my dad.'

'I'm sorry Karen.'

'You killed my dad and all you can say is sorry.' Karen spotted a gun underneath some of the papers in the drawer. She quickly grabbed it. 'Bye Mark.' *Pow.* She just killed her husband, but she wasn't going to jail. *Bang.*

Vanessa Opolot (12)
Trinity Catholic High School, Woodford Green

The Part Of Me I Never Knew?

I lived in a normal street in a normal town. I lived a normal life but unordinary things and past secrets opened the unordinary box that has always existed inside me. We moved house on the 6th month on the 6th day. Mother organised the whole thing, she wanted a change, from the chaotic city we lived in.

Mother told us that the new house is in the country and had 100 years of history. When I first caught sight of it thoughts ran through my mind. It was very dreary and the only sign of previous life was a stranded ball. Mother started with the names again 'cursed faith' or 'scar face'.

The more I got taunted the less time I spent at home.

Things at home changed. Mother's skeleton body changed into a plump shape; she was bearing a child. As the baby's arrival grew near, Billy and I grew closer. It was as if he felt the resentment I feel every single day of my life. On the 8th month of the 8th day I was ordered to get the baby stuff out of the loft. While in there I saw my baby box. As I opened it amazement struck me. Hot tears streamed down my face. It was like some past unknown spectrum reviling the truth.

I was a Siamese.

On the back was Mother's scrawny writing:

'Faith and Hope born 6/9/92.

Hope died 3/5/93'.

The feeling inside me was unexplainable. Turning away, I saw her, my twin sister …

Carlene Campbell (15)
Trinity Catholic High School, Woodford Green

I Don't Know What Came Over Me

I am trapped in a broken lift in John Lewis, just me and him. He is an odd-looking bloke; just standing and staring at me as though he is looking through me. He is a tramp; scruffy clothes, rucksack and his goldfish, yes, two little goldfish in a clear plastic bag, like when you win them at a fair.

The lift has been stopped for fifteen minutes now, and I regret coming - I had planned to grab something for my mum's birthday on my way home from work. I stand there looking back at this fish guy when he asks me if I have any water; then suddenly he rips open the bag and water and fish are sent flying all over the place.

So this guy is deranged, his fish are clearly dead so he just sits down in the corner. Then he looks up at me, his eyes glaze over and he shouts, *'It's all your fault!'* He runs at me. Adrenaline kicks in; suddenly I am fighting this crazy man and it feels good. He gets up after another hit and we clash again. He falls. He won't get up this time. I can sense it - I can see it - the body is on the floor: dead.

I could only tell them, 'I don't know what came over me,' but they didn't listen, and all I have left now is a tiny cell that will be my home until the day I die, and two goldfish.

Tom McGuire (15)
Trinity Catholic High School, Woodford Green

All I Can See

The girl picked up her pen and started to write.

'I am a willow tree. I was very lonely, in the garden. I didn't like the other flowers. They were too vain. I was happy when the rose was planted. I remembered it from a bud. It had white petals with pretty pink tips. I remember how shy it was when I first talked to it. I helped it grow, parting my overhanging leaves for it to get sunlight and protecting it from the wind. I loved that rose. I watched it grow tall. I saw its soft silky pink petals open one morning into glorious deep red, making every other flower seem dull.

I can still see my rose being taken away from me. I saw as the bride passed all the other flowers just to have my rose. True the blood-red looked radiant against her clean white bride's dress. I wish she hadn't taken it. I watched as my rose fell from her dress as she danced on the cloudy night. It seemed an age to fall, as it hit the ground I saw the rain droplets running slowly down its petals. My rose wept for its life.

And now, today, I am still here but the rose is not. I am full of joy though, I see a small shoot in exactly the same place my rose grew. And I know that little shoot will grow into something beautiful.

The girl put down her pen and smiled.

Genevieve Karacochi (14)
Trinity Catholic High School, Woodford Green

Respect

'Ryan, this isn't working anymore,' was the last thing Ryan ever thought he'd hear his girlfriend of nine months say to him as they approached her house.

Tears rolled down his snow-pale cheeks as he trudged up the steep hill towards his house, over and over in his head he thought of all the possibilities that his ex-girlfriend could have had, 'I don't get girls!'

As soon as the words left his mouth he knew something strange had happened, a circle of pink smoke surrounded him and the sweet smell of feminine perfume filled the air. A high-pitched shriek pierced through the air as Ryan saw what had happened to him, he didn't know how or why it had happened but one thing he did know was that he was in the body of a girl.

On Ryan's first day at school as a girl he not only had boys whistling at him, he'd had other students ask for his number all day, and had noticed that many of the other boys in the year had been treating him with no respect at all, but more as eye candy.

It was clear to Ryan after going through this in just one day what girls had to put up with. He promised himself that he would never again treat anyone with any less respect than what they deserved. As soon as these thoughts passed through his mind, blue smoke surrounded him in a circle and the smell of sweat and aftershave filled the air around him.

Phoebe Anthony (15)
Trinity Catholic High School, Woodford Green

Mission Impossible

There I was, in space, trying to deactivate a high-powered laser that could destroy a whole city in one shot. To make things even worse it was highly radioactive so the radiation would affect the whole planet and the wildlife. Whilst I was trying to deactivate the laser, the Mafia boss who had created the laser was floating towards me with a machete.

He shouted to me, 'Take this, Max, hahahahahahahahaha.'

Then I said back, 'Why do you always create mayhem when I am on holiday?'

He swung at me but I pulled out the wire that would deactivate the laser, he cut that instead. Then, instead of the machine breaking down, it started to count down and the boss said, 'We have ten seconds before the machine blows up and well, let's just say we have ten seconds to get out.'

I replied, 'Why do your machines always have some way of killing me?'

'I always know you are going to destroy my machines so I have to have a back up plan,' he said.

While he was talking, I found where the escape pod was, he didn't notice until I shouted, 'Yes, I've found it. 3, 2 …

I wished every second that it would stop but it just counted to 1 then *kaboom!* The pod just shot out, the force of the laser was so powerful, I couldn't move a muscle. A voice kept saying 'Temperature is 200c.' Then I collapsed.

Christopher Mansbridge (12)
Trinity Catholic High School, Woodford Green

A Day In The Life Of A Depressed Person

It was a dark night. Amy was lying on her bed writing in her diary, thinking about the marks on her arms, how she wished more than anything that today never happened.

24th June 2006

How could I have let this happen? I thought Olivia was going to kill me, she saw my arms …

'What's that?' said Olivia

'What?' I looked at my arms and saw the scars from the night before. 'Oh nothing, come on, let's go.'

… She wouldn't shut up about it, I thought she might even tell someone. I ended up confessing everything to her, how I felt so bad, like a failure, and how I just couldn't take it any longer …

'You should tell someone,' Olivia said, concerned about me.

'I can't,' I replied quietly.

Olivia carried on questioning me. 'Why not?'

'You don't understand,' I cried, and walked off feeling angry and upset that even my best friend didn't understand.

… Olivia told me to tell someone how I felt, but she just doesn't understand, no one would understand, they would just judge me if I told people how I wanted to die and how the only way the pain will go is by cutting my arms, the sting in my arms is better than the pain I feel inside. I guess I'll have to wait and see … and hope Olivia doesn't tell.

Well I should go to bed now, today was a bad day, I hope tomorrow will be better.

Amy.

Catherine Watling (15)
Trinity Catholic High School, Woodford Green

Spookerlitteley Villiey Town

It was late at night and Harvey Lettifield was just coming home late from work. He had a very important job in the community, he was a policeman. (Known to the police as Sergeant Lettifield). He was extremely tired.

As he slowly turned the key in the door padlock and entered the house, he questioned. 'Honey where are you?' He walked into the living room where she usually was, she was not there. He searched in the kitchen. She was surprisingly there, lying on the table, dead.

He slowly turned in shock, as on the mirror it read: 'We know who you are, and we are out to get you'.

Scaredly he ran to his car unlocked the door, he jumped in and raced off to find a hotel. As he arrived at the Quimby hotel, he entered the building, he asked the lady at the counter the price to stay the night. The woman turned around for him not to find a woman but a ghost.

He ran along the corridor, he saw bloodstains on the carpet covering the entrance and the walls, next to the bloodstain was a dead body lying on the ground.

Racing to the lift he finally entered and a shiver ran down his spine now he was completely scared, on that day he did not only lose his beautiful wife but he was left in a zombie hotel. He pressed number four on the lift and went into the first hotel room he saw.

The window was open, so he looked outside. Then he looked behind him to find a bloodsucking vampire. The vampire said, 'You are one of us now, you are a chosen one, you are unique.'

I bet you haven't realised, the mirror words were not referring to Harvey, they were referring to you!

Nicole Farrell (11)
Trinity Catholic High School, Woodford Green

Demon

The sky was a mixture of dark purple and black, the sun was non-existent.

The almost complete family soon reached home and sat in front of the television after arriving home from school. They all agreed to watch 'EastEnders'. Suddenly Damian noticed a black figure glide across the window. The TV went black and the lights cut out. While they sat almost expecting something to jump at them; Damian's little brother, Jordan, insisted that he heard talking in the cellar so their mother went downstairs to check that no one was there. Another figure crossed the window, the lights and TV came back on and it gradually got brighter outside.

Within minutes she was back again and took up her original seat in-between her two sons.

'Just a faulty mains switch,' she said, with a sigh of relief.

Damian wasn't convinced. 'I saw figures passing the window each time something happened.'

'So did I.'

Their knees were banging together so hard you could hear them.

'Oh we had you going there!' exclaimed their dad entering the room looking very proud and grinning broadly.

Jordan looked confused, 'But what about ...'

'Must have been a coincidence,' interrupted their mum, looking frightened.

'Or was it?' asked their dad, his grin disappearing.

The whole family sat in silence. Jordan remembered the story he'd written in class about a haunted house based on his family. Had it come to life? He forced himself not to believe it.

Myles John (11)
Trinity Catholic High School, Woodford Green

The Shocking Kidnap

Sam Downy was a normal boy, he liked playing with his friends.

It was the day of the terrible crime. Sam went out for his break time and he played hide-and-seek with a few of his friends. He went to go and count in the alleyway just near the end of the school. Then, when the headmaster strolled in through to his office, a man that nobody knew came sneaking through the gates just missing the security cameras. He walked straight over to Sam, lifted him up and then ran away with him under his arms.

After this happened the teachers in the school left and went after the kidnapper. Everyone was getting really upset and worried, because it was getting dark and no one had seen or heard from him. With the greatest luck the phone rang and, of course, the mother picked it up. The croaky and scary voice said, 'I want nine thousand pounds or your son will die.'

The mother agreed, anxiously she put the phone down and in a worried way she turned to her husband.

The man wanted quite a bit of money otherwise he wouldn't hand over the child. The family had left to give the man the money and get back their child.

The man was waiting on the bridge right on the other side because he may need the chance to run. In a polite manner the police officer said to him, 'We will give you the money and then you give us the young one.'

The police officer slid the suitcase across the bridge and then, when the man got the money, he let the child go and then tried to run away, but there were a bunch of police officers on the side he was going to get off, so instead of giving himself up to the police he ended up killing himself. It was too much for him to handle so he had to do it because he didn't want to go to prison.

The family got back to normal and there were no more interruptions ever again.

Joseph Rose (12)
Trinity Catholic High School, Woodford Green

9/11 A Passenger On A Plane

I would have never thought this day would have come. Planes usually crash if there's a technical fault, but that was not the case.

Two men wearing pitch-black suits came stumbling across towards the front of the gangway, they were heading in the direction of the pilot. My stomach churned with fright. I knew there was a problem. An air hostess shouting excessively down the gangway towards the control room, 'You two men sit down and remain seated!'

My heart kept beating fast, blood running down my veins, passengers were looking ahead observing to find out what the commotion was all about until disaster struck …

Fiona Ibeawuchi (14)
Trinity Catholic High School, Woodford Green

A Day In The Life Of A Paramedic on 7/7/05

The buzz of the alarm clock went off at 7am as normal in the Jones' household. Mr and Mrs Jones both got up, like a normal day. They ate breakfast together and Mr Jones drove his wife to the station. They said their goodbyes and he drove off to work.

Mr Jones worked in one of the busiest hospitals in London, as a paramedic. It was a normal day, but things were about to change.

He got a call to Kings Cross at 9am. It was an urgent call. He jumped in the ambulance and rushed to the station.

On arriving at Kings Cross, there was smoke, people and dust everywhere. He knew it was bad from the moment he laid eyes on the situation.

He jumped out of his ambulance and got straight to work. He didn't know what was going on but he had a job to do. Many needed treating and there was no time to stop. His colleagues had told him two other bombs had gone off elsewhere in London.

As the day passed, there were an endless number of patients to treat. It was about 6pm and he had just got a break. He hadn't thought about it but he hadn't had a call from his wife. He tried calling her, but no answer. So he went home.

Later on he got a phone call. He hoped it was his wife. but it was the police. They had some bad news …

Mary-Anne Murray (15)
Trinity Catholic High School, Woodford Green

A Day In The Life Of A Schizophrenic

Sleep, eat, exercise and talk day in and day out. This is what my life has become, but I can't take anymore. I knew from the minute I woke up what I would do. I could feel Joy's warmth in my hand almost as a reassuring gesture of what I needed to do. No longer was I going to sit around and be the puppet I wanted to be the puppeteer. The usual feeling of sickness, anxiousness and dizziness were unusually faded for once. Quickly checking that the coast was clear outside my room I made a body shape out of the spare sheets I had stolen the night before. I knew that voice was always out to help me. I made a run for it. I could taste freedom, I made a hasty exit. Joy snugly secure in my hand.

'We are almost there now, Joy, just a bit longer,' I whispered.

'I can tell, keep going,' she whispered back and those few words made me feel even more confident. I quickly made my way through the stark, cold hallways, which were winding out in front of me, like long white snakes trying to confuse me, but I knew where I was going, I'd been down these halls enough. Behind me there was some sort of commotion going on I could hear raised voices. There was the exit all lit up as if it were waiting for me, finally I was out. Schizophrenia they said I had, I doubt it.

Katherine Rogers (15)
Trinity Catholic High School, Woodford Green

Dog's Investigation

I got Waggy's lead and we went off for a walk. He had been barking, he was in need of a walk. As I made my way to the forest, I spotted an elderly man. He was giving me a strange look. At first I ignored it but whenever I looked behind me he was always there. I started to get worried so I walked faster.

Finally I arrived in the forest. I put the lead longer so Waggy could run a bit. I could hear footsteps behind me, they were getting faster, my heart started pounding. (I was scared.) I turned around, he went to stab me. I dropped the lead and ran. I looked behind me and there on the floor was Waggy lying cold, bloodied, *dead*. The man was gone! I immediately rang 999. The police arrived about 15 minutes after the attack.

'Alright, we will try as hard as we can to solve this,' said PC Plum.

I didn't care if this killer was dead or alive, as long as they caught him.

Two weeks pass …

(*ring, ring*) I quickly ran to answer the phone.

'Hello, I have some good news. We have found a man near to the scene of the attack, he had your dog's blood on his clothes.'

I said, 'Thank you so much, I'm glad you've found him.' I was so upset to think he'd killed my dog. Later on I found out the man had killed himself.

Sophie Webb (12)
Trinity Catholic High School, Woodford Green

The Boy Who Needed A Haircut

'Mum, my hair's stuck again,' whimpered Jack.

'Coming,' groaned Mum.

Jack was six years old. He had brown eyes, freckles and a cheeky smile. The only problem about Jack is that he has very, very long blonde hair.

'Why don't you just cut your hair?'

'Because when I grow up I want to be a rock star with long hair.'

'Well then if you want your hair to keep getting stuck, that's fine by me.'

'But, but Mum,' shouted Jack.

'No buts, just get your hair tied back and go to school.'

'How was school?' Mum said.

'Fine.'

'Your hair got stuck again, didn't it?'

'Yes, but that doesn't mean I want a haircut.'

'OK, whatever you say, Jack.'

'Jack, come down and have dinner.' Mum shouted.

'So tell me about school then, Jack.'

'Do I have to?'

'Yes!'

'I walked to school, my hair got stuck on a bike, a kite, a bus and a lamp post. At school it got stuck in my locker, in my desk and in-between my shoelace. Apart from all that, I had a great day. Thanks for asking, now if you need me I'll be up in my room doing my homework.'

Mum went to give Jack his hot chocolate.

'Sorry, Mum, I've thought about what you have said about me having a haircut, is that possible?'

'Of course.'

Next day Jack went to have a haircut.

'I love it Mum, I never want long hair again.'

Sigourney Tabe (11)
Trinity Catholic High School, Woodford Green

How Did It Happen?

It is dark outside. Only me and my mum at home. I am having a bath. My mum is watching TV. Noises coming from the loft. I sit in the bath freezing cold. I sing a nursery rhyme that I learnt in nursery today. 'Twinkle, twinkle, little star, how I wonder what you are, up above the world so high like a diamond in the sky ...'

I repeatedly sing the same nursery rhyme again and again. Then, *squeak*! The door opens. It sounds like someone grinding their nails on a blackboard. I get a shiver down my spine. I go to grab my towel, turn around then *bang*... the door is shut!

I open the door as slowly as I can. I look left then right ... nothing. I run up the stairs into her room but she isn't there either. This isn't a big house, we only have four rooms. 'Mum,' I call quietly, but no reply. I don't know what to do, where to go, or who to call. She isn't in the kitchen or any room either. The only place left is the bathroom, but I was just in there a minute ago. I go and check just in case.

Blood trails across the floor up the walls and into the bath ...

'Mum! Noooooooo!'

Lots of questions to be answered, who did it? How did they get in? Who knows?

Kellen Moniz (12)
Trinity Catholic High School, Woodford Green

Aromas

Once upon a time Aromas, a German knight, was on a ride with his horse. Aromas looked at the sky and thought to himself what a wonderful day it was. All of a sudden an arrow from behind struck his horse. The horse let out a loud screeching scream. The horse galloped away leaving Aromas on the floor. Out of nowhere the sky turned grey and a storm began to blow.

Again another arrow came and this time it missed.

Aromas saw someone in the distance. He chased after him with his sword out. He struck the man on the leg. The man got up and said, 'It is just the beginning,' and died.

Aromas looked up and saw his army behind him then he looked in front of him and saw about 4,000 English soldiers running at him. He got out his shield and ...

Joshua Porter (12)
Trinity Catholic High School, Woodford Green

The Disaster Of Christmas Morning

'This will be the first Christmas without Mum here,' Tod Jones said to his father.

'I know, son, but it will be the first Christmas with Ruby! Which is good,' said Tod's Dad, Alan. Ruby was Alan's girlfriend. She was horrible to Tod.

It was Christmas Eve and Ruby was being really mean to Tod. He was very excited about playing with the PSP Alan had promised him for Christmas.

Tod woke early on Christmas morning and ran to wake his Dad and Ruby. Dad handed him a present which was heavy and rectangular. *Strange,* thought Tod as he ripped the paper off.

'Oh,' said Tod when he saw an encyclopaedia about football.

'Yes, son,' said Alan. 'Ruby told me you'd changed your mind and now wanted this book. I'm really pleased we could give you something you really wanted.'

After breakfast Tod went to his room. He could not believe that woman had done something so terrible to him, he was heartbroken, and that's when he made his decision …

Boxing Day arrived and Alan thought it was strange that Tod had not woken by 11am, so he went to his room. He pulled back the covers on his bed and discovered a pile of pillows where Tod should have been.

Alan climbed in the car knowing where his son would be. He found Tod sitting by his mother's grave. 'Come home, son, we'll work things out, I promise.'

Molly Kerrigan (12)
Trinity Catholic High School, Woodford Green

Thin Ice!

I watched them whizzing past me, it was amazing the way they could jump and leap and twirl in the air. I wished to be like them one day, all the other girls at school did ballet or tap, but I wanted to be different, not the same, definitely not! That was when I decided to join, I used to love dancing and doing lifts with my partner, James, he never dropped me, not once, until one day, the day I shall never forget, it changed my life forever!

It all started when our performance instructor was giving us some great news. 'Right now, everyone, we have been selected to broadcast our own show on ice! Everyone in the school will be taking part, the show will be shown in three weeks time so we need to practise each and every day, so come on, let's get started!'

Everyone was so excited, we all had different parts to do and me, well I had the best. Me and James we were the stars of the show. We would perform the triple spin, in the finale, the most dangerous lift that anyone could do. But I wasn't scared, not with James as my partner. I could jump off the tallest building ever and he would still catch me, oh but how wrong was I!

In rehearsals we did the lift to perfection, every twist, every spin, every catch was done in such a graceful manner, we were sure to dazzle everyone who watched.

'Right now, it's a big day tomorrow, so I want you all to get a good night's sleep and I want you to be here at 7am on the dot.' So I went home and got the well-deserved rest so I could face the crowds in the morning.

The day finally came, I was so excited I rushed down to the rink and waited for the audience to arrive. The time came for me to perform. I stood right behind the curtain and waited for them to be opened, finally they were. All the bright lights shone into my eyes but that would never stop me from dancing, then disaster struck, when James prepared for the final catch, he slipped on the glazed ice. I came tumbling down, I tried to land on my feet but as James slipped, his skate flung off and the blade hit me right in my leg hurling me to the ground!

The ambulance came and took us both to hospital. James was fine, but me, well the hospital said that I would be in a wheelchair for as long as it would take, and many years on I am still sitting beside the rink, like I did before, but this time wishing I'd never started performing.

Louise Jarvis (12)
Trinity Catholic High School, Woodford Green

Mondays

I came down to breakfast, as usual I was still tired from staying up late. I hadn't even done my homework for the next day. I arrived at school and I spotted one of my friends and went over to him. He was chatting away to Pete, 'What are you talking about?'

'When I arrived at school, there was this big black limo like the American President has,' said Pete.

'Then you won't believe this Zack, but President Bush walked into the school,' said Josh.

I couldn't believe it! Just then the bell rang. I made my way to class when our head teacher appeared called Mr Peters. 'All to the hall please we've got an assembly.'

So I turned around confused, like everyone else, and made my way to the hall and I sat down.

'Hush please,' said Mr Peters. 'Now the reason I called this assembly is because when I arrived at school today I found a letter in my study. It was from an important person asking whether they could take a post at our school. This is because I am retiring.' Everyone gasped. 'That person is President Bush.'

'Good morning, now I'm a bit like you. I hate getting up on a Monday morning, I want to lie in don't you?'

'Yes,' chanted everyone.

'Don't you think school should start later?'

'Yeah!'

'And I think school should end later!'

'Exactly!' shouted Tom.

And ever since that Monday, I've actually enjoyed going to school, especially on Mondays.

Stephen Wasmuth (12)
Trinity Catholic High School, Woodford Green

Maciver - The English Tyrant

A Scottish knight named Maciver stood alone at the gate of his baron's castle as a key to the battle. He was feared by all but still men thought they could overcome him as they approached him. Hundreds lay before him that he cut down. Men started to retreat as he thought the battle was won, but on came catapults. As they struck the castle a rock struck Maciver in the head, knocking him unconscious.

'Where am I?' Maciver asked. A monk stood there.

'Ah, you have finally awoken, the king wishes to see you,' the monk answered.

'King? Where am I?' Maciver said sternly.

'King Edward,' the monk replied again. 'Come on, let's go.'

Maciver faced the king and said, 'I need fresh air, we shall talk outside.'

The king gritted his teeth and walked to the gate. Edward ordered, 'I have finally captured you Maciver, now you will serve me or *die!* Knowing you're smart, I know which one you will choose.'

Maciver smashed Edward in the face taking his sword, opening the gate, he ran back to Scotland.

Six months on …

'Men, this battle shall seal Edward's fate, *charge!*' Maciver shouted, breaking through the gate and charging to Edward.

Edward was drunk from the night before and in no state to fight. Edward woke and reached for his blade, but it was too late. He pleaded for his life, as Maciver criticised him but he barked back and was killed.

'Let's go, my task is complete.'

John Barker (12)
Trinity Catholic High School, Woodford Green

Little War Hero

I looked up at my brother - that crimson-faced schoolboy that chuckled and chewed the end of his pencil seemed a long way off now. Donny looked like a man. I didn't like it.

'That uniform looks silly.' I frowned. Nobody took any notice of me. My mother was too busy weeping and my father was giving my brother a lecture on the conduct of a good soldier. I crumpled into a heap on the sofa hiding my face with my straight, waist-length blonde hair. It wasn't fair!

Finally, after what seemed like an eternity, I felt a light tap on my shoulder. I lifted my head to see my brother towering above me. His muddy-brown hair was slicked back with gel so that his face looked hard and scary. He knelt down on the floor so that his eyes looked straight into mine. His were sparkling full of tears. Immediately the hard image was broken; he wasn't really like that underneath. How would he ever survive a war?

'Bye little sis,' he whispered. And that was the last I thought I'd ever see of him.

It was during those long six years of World War II that I grew up, and although I'm ashamed to say it, I almost forgot about my brother. His face was but a tattered photograph in the far corners of my memory. Then, on my sixteenth birthday, he returned. I threw my arms around him and smiled.

'That uniform does not look silly.'

Siobhan Lyons (12)
Trinity Catholic High School, Woodford Green

The Lady Of Arcady

'Who is she?' can be heard a thousand times in the hustling and bustling crowds of Camden, as a pale, thin and forlorn girl enters the romantic realm of Arcadia, her glazed eyes attracting many a man.

'She is the Lady of Arcady,' states a wise old fellow. 'Brought here by the poppy, opium, the flower of dreams.' And as his mutterings turn into ramblings, the lady breaks the hearts she stole form the men that loved her, and into them she etches melancholy. Those men are now shivering in the rain like lost sparrows with no direction home.

The Lady of Arcady is blessed by a faded and jaded beauty, which has been scarred by unthinkable sins, yet sins that have been thought of. But however heartless she may be, she is the 'Doomed Generation's' only hope. Without her there would be no one to stand against the patronising politicians to fight for freedom, to keep the nostalgia and pride there in our ghoulish souls. The slits in the sky may glare right through us like gouging eyes, but we stand strong against the searing stare.

We have waited two thousand years to break the walls and puzzles that surround us, and lo and behold, we have. The lady has arrived in Arcady and finally Albion's defences are here; poetry, literature and sweet determination.

Sonny Brown (12)
Trinity Catholic High School, Woodford Green

Jeopardising The Truth

I know I should never have told them. They didn't deserve to know. The Egyptians have stolen our way of life all because of me.

At the late hours of the day I had the great honour of serving at the feast in remembrance of those who came from above! From the kitchen window I saw the twin volcanoes shaking violently. The ground began thumping like my beating pulse. Poisonous thick black smoke clogged the land. The sound of screaming citizens had faded and by now the building was toppling! It was so sudden! I found a window and jumped to what I thought was my death!

I woke up, I had been rescued and within a few weeks I was amongst the wondrous reaches of Egypt. But was Atlantis really gone? The people were very welcoming although this didn't bring out the best of me.

Twenty years before the death of my parents, some 'visitors' came to Atlantis. These visitors lived very different lives and showed us that, by bending space, time and light we could move huge rocks on top of one another. Thanks to me the Egyptians now use this method for their pyramids. The visitors asked us never to reveal these secrets or else! We respected them by using their language for signs. Again, because of me, the Egyptian sign of protection is almost identical to one of the visitor's crop circles.

I was told by the Egyptians this was old news. I was just consolidating 'twenty-year-old' marvels. I was not the destroyer of Atlantis!

Max Wells (12)
Trinity Catholic High School, Woodford Green

Gladiator

'Argh!' A powerful swing from the lethal blade of the first slave sliced through the tense arm of the innocent stranger put before him; the blood-drenched limb hit the floor, still clenching the spear. The slave followed, collapsing dead.

Another victory for Marcus Tiberius, fighting every hour of every day slaughtering every man or animal placed before him.

Until, one day, Marcus met his match: Augustus was tired of Marcus continually thrashing every 'contestant' put in front of him, so he travelled to a Greek island: rumours had reached Rome, and Augustus wanted to find out how true those rumours were...

A week later, when Emperor Augustus returned, it was a great shock to Marcus, when he was presented with another challenge, although he did not know who or what he was up against.

The creaking of the colossal, iron gates through the pierced holes in Marcus' helmet made him even more nervous, and when he stepped into the arena, it was not long before he met his opponent.

'Warrgh!' a fist of granite smacked into Marcus' face forcing him onto the hard, dusty ground.

The warrior drew his battle-scarred sword and thrust it into Marcus' stomach, piercing his armour, and then again, this time into his right arm. The sounds and screams in the stadium were no longer sounds and screams to Marcus, but pain and agony. For one final time, the warrior's immense sword was jerked from his victim's gory arm and straight into Marcus' suffering heart.

Jack Herring (12)
Trinity Catholic High School, Woodford Green

The Perfect Holiday

Easter holiday 2006 we went to the Algarve, Portugal. The reason this particular holiday has become special to me, is because my dad had a surprise planned for us.

Three days into the holiday Dad got up early and told us the taxi was going to pick us up.

'Oh no,' I said, 'not more shopping!'

'Just hurry up and let's go.'

It was only a 15-minute ride and from a distance I could see a huge board with *'Zoomarine'* on it.

'Come on,' said Dad. 'You are going to like this.'

When we went in the staff took a family photo which we could buy on the way out. An instructor came and booked me and my sister in for the swimming with dolphins session. After this we had three hours to walk around the park and see different animals.

We saw shows like the seals, parrots, there were also many rides. We had a light lunch of chicken piri-piri. At 3pm the instructors came and took us to change into our wetsuits. They gave us a lesson on dolphins and what we should do. Then our family could come in and watch us swim with them. We had a choice, we could hold their fins or the dolphins could push us out of the water with their noses. We had a water fight with them and learnt how to do tricks.

It was a fantastic experience, and one I will come to do again but for now we have photos and a DVD of the day, and when I watch it, it reminds me of my perfect holiday.

Antonio Delle Grazie (13)
Trinity Catholic High School, Woodford Green

Legend Of The Silent Assassin

I will tell you a tale of murder, deception and woe. A long time ago in Kansas a man called Smith Thomson took out a loan to enter a poker tournament. He ended up losing the tournament and went bust, he could not pay back the money he owed to the richest man in the state at that time, Billy Kid.

Because he could not pay the money he turned to violence, robbery and murder. He robbed the ranch town bank and emptied its safe but this didn't dent the amount of money he owed to Kid. Thomson was so bad and now infamous he made a lot of enemies especially Kid himself, which usually meant death. One day Smith was asleep in his brother's house when three armed men barged in and shot his brother thinking it was him. They cut out his tongue, beat him up and gouged a X into his neck. They left him to die in a pool of his own blood.

From that day forward Smith vowed that he would never pass through the gates of Saint Peter, he had to avenge his brother's death. He found one of the men and planted three bullets in his head while he slept and wrote in his blood on the wall 'the silent assassin'. From that day forth a tale spread about this elusive silent assassin and anyone that said a bad word about him usually ended up dead.

Smith eventually killed the three men, his last and only target was Billy Kid. By this time Kid was an old man but he was still massively respected and many people served under him.

One day Smith crept into Kid's house without a sound and sneaked across the courtyard to stand underneath a balcony. He climbed a vine and got onto the balcony that led to Kid's private chamber. Kid was in the bath. Smith walked in and dunked Kid's head under the water then shot him in the head. His life's work now done he turned the gun on himself to end his tortured life.

Kyle Milligan (12)
Trinity Catholic High School, Woodford Green

Untitled

Left, right, left, right …

I thought it was beginning to rain, but I realised it was sweat, dripping slowly from my forehead! I looked down to my feet where the ball still was …

'Sang!'

'Sang!'

My fellow football team members were all screaming my name to pass the ball to them. I looked to my right … and to my left again.

'Sang! What the hell are you doing? Pass the ball!' I could hear my football coach shouting at me as I fell to the floor. My eyes slowly shut and my last vision was the goalkeeper, Luke, peering down at me …

I woke up in a hospital bed. I was so confused. Why was I here? What had happened? 'Hi there, Sang. I'm your nurse, Sally!'

Why am I here? I wondered and then asked her.

'You fainted on the football pitch. You were rushed to hospital, and you have just had a quick operation but you should be able to return home tomorrow morning.'

'Good because I need to play the final this weekend!' I smiled and decided to just rest and relax while I had the chance.

'Ohhh no you won't,' said the nurse. 'No more football for you for at least a month!'

My smile turned quickly to a frown. I saw my life flash before my eyes and my football career. Everything I had worked for was now useless and wasted … I had played through the whole FA Cup and now it was the final and I couldn't even play it.

I decided I would leave … run out of the hospital … and I would play the game if it was the last thing I did …

Sang Vu (13)
Trinity Catholic High School, Woodford Green

The Last House On The Street

The house at the end of Elm Street has been derelict for around 13 years. The last owners moved out rather hurriedly, leaving much of their furniture and possessions. Yet none of the youths had attempted to explore it, or rob it. It's a forbidding place. The lifeless trees around the old house are stark - no birds have ever rested anywhere near them. Squirrels and rabbits are startled by passing cars and run away, only to stop suddenly as they see the house. Cats screech and arch their backs anywhere near it. Dogs suddenly slump down and pine - until their owner takes them away.

There is a rumour that the local children speak of, a rumour of the one person ever to enter the house. A boy called Chris supposedly entered the house for a dare. There are no ideas to what he saw, but he is said to have gone completely insane. The parents encourage this story to prevent their offspring causing trouble in the house, but the fact that at the other end of the road their lives a half sane old man is enough proof for the children.

The odd thing is the house is otherwise entirely normal. No horrific murders, no Indian burial ground. Not a spectral sausage. The only sign of anything weird is that the last digit in the house number (669) has come loose. The upside down nine now ends, the number is 666. The sign of the beast.

Joseph Browning (14)
Trinity Catholic High School, Woodford Green

Area 54

On an island in the middle of the ocean, a man called James Mitchell stood looking for human civilisation. His boat had run out of fuel and had crashed into some rocks. His only chance of survival rested in his survival instincts.

James was a well-trained man dressed in full dark leather. He was usually a brave man but something was off …

Mist brewed in the air, the sky started to get dark. The island came alive with strange sounds and movements. James thought it was best to look for shelter.

Running through the meek jungle, trees and bushes he vaguely spotted a rundown building. He went to inspect the building and he noticed that it was in fact a research facility that looked like it had been abandoned a long time ago.

The building was in bad shape. The windows were smashed and cracked, the front doors looked like they had been smashed out. Grime and vines covered a glass dome-like structure and doors.

He was starting to get scared. He walked up to the doors and continued inside. James was now breathing hard and took each step slowly trying to tell himself that there was nothing there.

As soon as James came to terms with what was happening, he realised that he had cut himself on a test tube that had been smashed beforehand. A clattering noise made him jump. James was as scared as ever, he felt like a little child who had just had a scary dream. He had mutated.

Matthew Edmunds (14)
Trinity Catholic High School, Woodford Green

Proterozoic Returns

The year was 2056 AD - last time I checked. Though I'm sure nobody knows the year any longer.

About 20 years ago, the sun's gravitational force weakened severely and its tight grip on Earth was lost. Earth continues to drift further back from the sun and temperatures continue to plummet. The continental ice plates have spread, causing a second Ice Age, but this time it will not diminish, just render the Earth uninhabitable.

At the time of the 'big freeze', there was a huge rush to migrate to the inhabitable country, Ecuador, meaning equator. The huge panic to get there saw huge air congestion, many planes crashed under the extreme temperatures; mine was one of them. My plane crashed and fell just short of a small ice plate. I presume it to be an ice plate and not Ecuador, as I haven't seen a single person since I have been here - well not until now …

Suddenly, there are thousands of people populating this once empty, islet-like ice plate. My relief is incomprehensible, after all these decades, to see another human feels incredible. But thus far, none have noticed me, not even after I address them. Their hoods cover their faces and nothing can be seen beyond the deep black; this, a metaphor for their ambiguity. Humans weren't like this, were they? Have I developed my own language after all these years? Am I a spectre? Are they?

Extreme hallucinations are experienced in the first stage of hypothermia, some say. This of course, being death.

Colin Currie (14)
Trinity Catholic High School, Woodford Green

The Wind That Blew North

It was just the 2nd December and it is a cold winter's evening, you see I am an orphan, I have not had parents practically my whole life. I am cold as I sleep in a cellar at the bottom of my foster mother's house. I have lived with her since I was bought in to Social Services. Gertrude Billabong is her name, her saying is, 'New Orphans expect better treatment.' I am an old orphan, and I am no one.

It has been ten years since I have stepped on my own two feet; I am somebody in this world. I now work in management for a top company in London, called IQ. It is a great place this world since I have left Billabong Services. In my fantasy world I think I am just like Anastasia, leaving her orphanage, being sent into the big world by herself knowing no one. Her life was exactly the same as mine, pitiful and heartbreaking.

I am now in my thirties, you know the saying, 'Thirty and thriving', and I am loving it. My life is back on track since I have found out the truth about my parents, you see the story was that they had separated and neither of them wanted me as they were too young. I got over it, they didn't want me, but somebody does, that is my fiance Luke, he has held my hand in every single moment of my messed up life.

Margaret McGillicuddy (13)
Trinity Catholic High School, Woodford Green

Street Car 13

For the past five days Jessica had become more certain that she was being followed; only the other day she had seen a tall gentleman staring at her, he was wearing a hat which reminded her of those worn by detectives. Since then he had caught the same street cars to the south of the city, and had even been sitting in a car outside her house.

On the morning of June 22nd she was travelling home from school when her street car was hijacked by a group of men, one of whom she instantly recognised as her 'spy'. Before she had a chance to scream, a chloroform-soaked rag was being held over her mouth ...

When Jessica came to she did not know how long it had been since the incident in the number 13 street car. *Half an hour or so?* she thought. She looked up and saw three men staring down at her, all three were wearing three-piece suits.

'What do we do with her now, Foxy?' said a fat man smoking a cigar.

'We get her to talk!' replied another, who Jessica assumed was Foxy.

'Yeah, I can't wait to get some answers out of her,' chuckled the spy.

'Shut it Roger!' shouted Foxy. 'Now Miss. All we want to know is which bank your father keeps his millions in? Once you have told us you are free to ...'

Wham! Jessie brought the chair down on Foxy's head, and keyed 911 into her mobile, she would never betray her father.

When the police arrived they locked up the gangsters and told her there was a reward. 'These are dangerous criminals, it's amazing you got away.'

'It was nothing,' she lied.

Kristian Zarebski (13)
Trinity Catholic High School, Woodford Green

A Day In The Life ...

My first memories are of waking in the dirt and bacteria which was all around me. I lived in a council flat in Hackney, East London. My life was tough and with my mum as useless as a fish, there really was no escape. My dad was a vicious bully. He hurt me and my baby sister Dawn for pleasure, and he hurt my mum too. My mum didn't do anything to stop it though and she did as she was told.

I spent my childhood days wandering around the streets. My dad didn't want me in the house and he just didn't care. I wandered for hours a day and waited until it turned dark when I was allowed home. I starved myself and I would do anything to try and feed Dawn. I was a pigeon, a scavenger, taking anything I could get my dirty little hands on. I would sometimes go to visit my auntie, who was the closest person I could call family.

I had nothing in my childhood life; no one to love, no family, no food, no drink, nothing! Everything bad always happened to me, and the surroundings didn't help either.

Every day before I went to sleep, I wished and imagined what my life could be ... what I wished it would be! I wished that Dawn and I could live with Auntie, and be happy with food, drink and most importantly ... have someone to love us!

Ella Faulkner (13)
Trinity Catholic High School, Woodford Green

A Day In The Life Of Becky

Surrounded by my seven brothers and sisters, I wouldn't say it was boring. Chasing, playing, fighting, there is never a dull moment. Here comes the lady that Mum calls our nanny, she feeds us, washes us and plays with us. Oh no, she is not alone. Ever since we were babies there were people coming in and playing with us. They used to play with us all but now specific couples only play with one of us. The people that have just arrived play with me.

They pick me up but this time they don't put me down on the ground but in a car. What's happening to me?

'Mum!' I shout through the shut window. My heart is thumping. I can't see any of my brothers or sisters, or my mummy. I'm scared. The car stars to move. The people in the front start talking to me, it sounds as though they are telling me I am going to live with them and they are going to be my mummy and daddy. I don't need them. I have a mummy although I hadn't seen my daddy in ages.

The car stops and I reach a large house, not knowing if it's safe, I look around. I wet myself.

The house is big and I feel lost. In the corner of the kitchen there is a cage with a bed in it. The woman starts calling me 'Becky' and tries to tickle my tummy. Two young people come in. 'Grandma, you've got a puppy.'

Katherine Dadswell (13)
Trinity Catholic High School, Woodford Green

Dungreen Castle

Has anyone ever told you the story of Dungreen Castle? I advise you if you don't like ghosts to put the book down now. Well, continuing, I am about to tell you a story of the scariest castle in Great Britain. This castle was a well-respected home for the almighty King Goethe. He was an evil king who killed people for no reason. Everyone hated him and everyone was pleased when he was killed one night. He was killed by a dagger in the back. No one ever knew who did this.

Ever since the king died many reports have been forwarded to ghost catchers. People have spent nights there and had to get therapy. They said they've heard a ghost singing in the corridor. One man said he'd actually seen the ghost. He said he was very tall with old, grand clothes on. The castle has been deserted for over 65 years now. No one has the courage to enter the ghost trap.

The last man that visited the castle said he will never be able to sleep again. The ghost of Dungreen Castle said he will never stop haunting people, according to the last visitors.

A few years ago, a very brave man thought he would check the castle out. He brought a camcorder with him so everybody could see what he'd done. He stayed one night there. Throughout the night he heard someone singing a very old song. He thought he would check it out. He went out into the corridor and saw a very tall figure with an axe. The camcorder cut out and we never saw the man again!

Liam Cooper (13)
Trinity Catholic High School, Woodford Green

A Day In The Life Of …

I happily swam in the deep blue sea, until something happened. Something that had never happened to me before. I had heard rumours of it, but I never thought they were true. I was taken up by the sky, steam and wind. I was with many others of my kind, they seemed relaxed about it, but being young, I was frightened to death.

It all happened so fast it was almost a total blur to me. When it ended I was in a totally different world. Large animals moving above me, making it as if they couldn't see me at all. All of the others who were with me when were taken up, were now forming a bond together, so they would not get separated. I joined the bond.

Though it might not have been the smartest thing to do, because shortly after I joined the bond, we were soon separated. Some of the smaller animals who were above us, came down with full force. Splitting us up without a care in the world. I flew faraway from the group and ended up, in a dark, deep place. It wasn't pleasant at all.

I went through many things that I had never come across before, in my life. This was a part of the rumour that I thought was 100% made up, now I knew I was wrong. Will I ever get home to tell the rumour? To tell the story?

Parris Francis (12)
Trinity Catholic High School, Woodford Green

I'm Not Martin!

'I'm not Martin, I'm not Martin!'

'Of course you are,' said the nurse, in an annoyed and exhausted tone.

'Come on stop hassling me.'

'Sshh, you need to be quiet. There's a new patient next to you and he's very nervous and he doesn't need you shouting the place down, anyway you're not the only person here.'

'Are you sure you're alright?'

'Yes Mum,' replied Kevin. 'I'm a little nervous, that's all!'

'You'll be fine son,' I know you will.'

'Yeah you're right, thanks Dad,' said Kevin.

'Are you sure you have everything?'

'Yes Mum,' said Kevin rolling his eyes, 'I've got enough socks to last me a lifetime!'

The tannoy came on and said that visiting time was over, the nurse came over and said, 'I'm afraid it's that time.'

'Oh no, come on then one last hug.'

'Okay ewww, ouch, ow Mum!'

'Oh sorry, I'll be back tomorrow, sleep tight.'

'Yeah get a good night's sleep, you've got a big operation tomorrow son. I will see you soon, bye.'

Kevin was sitting up in bed taking in his surroundings; the plain green walls, the kiddie pictures up everywhere, then he noticed the strange boy in the bed next to him, above his headboard was a sign with his name on, it read: *Martin Ross*.

Kevin was bored so he tried to make conversation with him. 'Er ... hello ... it's Martin isn't it?'

'I'm not Martin!' he shouted.

'Oh I'm sorry, it's just it says Martin on that sign.'

'Well I'm not Martin,' he said coldly. 'So what you in for?' he said without looking at Kevin.

'Oh I'm having my appendix out.'

'Lucky you,' he said.'

'Why, what are you having done?'

'I'm having my leg removed.'

'Oh my God, I'm so sorry.'

'Well don't be,' he replied back quietly, 'because I'm not having it done.'

'Huh?' What do you mean?'

He didn't answer.

The lights went out and Martin just sat there with his arms crossed while Kevin on the other hand was shattered and went to sleep as soon as his head hit the pillow.

During the night Kevin suddenly awoke, two men came to the end of his bed muttering to each other quietly, then one of them said, 'Right let's get Martin.'

The other said, 'Who's that?'

'That kid who's having his leg removed,' then they started moving Kevin's bed.

'What are you doing?' demanded Kevin. 'Where are you taking me?'

'Come on Martin, pipe down or you'll wake everyone up.'

'I'm not Martin!'

'Yep, they said you'd say that,'

Then Kevin knew what had happened. Martin had switched the names above the beds.

'No!'

Martin sat up, smiled and waved goodbye to Kevin.

Kevin screeched at the top of his lungs, *'I'm not Martin!'*

Alex Sawinski (13)
Trinity Catholic High School, Woodford Green

The Journey To Youth

On Tuesday morning Beth, of 79 years, was getting ready to do her two hours in the charity shop. As she was heading out of the door, the postman gave her a letter, she put it in her bag and went to work. Later she took out the letter, it read:

'Dear Beth,

Tomorrow at 12pm a boat will leave from Portsmouth Harbour, please be there to board.

Yours sincerely,

A friend.'

When Beth was reading the letter she was gobsmacked, but she just walked up the stairs and packed her bag.

She arrived at Portsmouth the next day and boarded the boat. Seven days later she arrived at an island.

Everyone started to walk so Beth followed. As she was walking she looked at her hands and to her amazement they didn't have any wrinkles. From her pocket she took out her mirror, as she pulled it up to her face she saw a younger version of herself. Beth thought she must be dreaming so she pinched herself to wake up, but it wasn't a dream.

Soon they came to a clearing, a man started to speak, he said, 'You have two choices one is to stay on the island and be young forever, or get on the boat, back to your normal lives.' The only condition was that once they'd made their choice there was no going back.

Each week Beth watched the boat come to the island with new people, a few did get on and go back.

Hayley Donovan (13)
Trinity Catholic High School, Woodford Green

Why Me?

Why me? Nina thought to herself, she was being picked on again, being strange. At least it was home time in a couple of minutes, she had locked herself in the toilets until the bell rang.

Nina rushed out, caught the first bus and rushed into her house. It was the only place she felt safe. It was like walking into another world.

'Hello darling,' said Mum, who was feeding Nina's younger sister, Lisa.

'Hi,' Nina said, as she ran up into her bedroom. As soon as she reached her bedroom she grabbed her laptop and checked her emails. A rush of happiness filled her body. Her best friend, Katie, who lived in Australia had sent her an email. Nina started to read it but her eyes began to water with unhappiness because Katie wrote that they wouldn't be able to write to each other anymore because her dad had lost his job and couldn't afford it.

Why me? Nina thought to herself, she went downstairs crying.

'What's wrong?' Mum asked.

Nina explained and her mum said she could phone, but she knew that it wouldn't be the same as she wouldn't be allowed to use it.

'What am I going to do?' Nina asked Mum.

'We will talk after dinner,' she replied.

When Nina went back up to her room, she emailed Katie back to explain how she felt. Then Nina's Mum came in with a smile on her face.

'Nina how about going to Australia for a holiday?' said Mum.

The happiness came straight back and filled Nina's body.

Amy Wybrant (13)
Trinity Catholic High School, Woodford Green

The Seven Doors

She looked up at the mountain that lay before her … She lifted her foot and wedged it into the snow of the thick, tall mountain. Then she lifted her hand to grip it. As her hand touched the snow, a cold shiver went down her spine. She started to climb.

After a while she had reached halfway. As the snow fell down, her eyesight blurred, she couldn't look up anymore, she didn't know how much longer there was to go … but she sensed that she was nearly there. She had reached the clouds. Only a few feet until the top. She moved her hand upwards, trying to feel for the edge. As she found the flat surface she pulled herself up. She tried to stand.

She started to crawl to the other side of the mountain. Her feet were at the edge now. She looked down. It was steep. She stood up. The ocean lay at the bottom.

Suddenly, a strong gust of wind knocked her balance … her feet left the edge of the mountain. Now her whole body fell through the air, and through the clouds. The air brushed past her face as she fell.

The ocean hit her like a brick wall. She was sinking … deeper and deeper … into nothingness. Everything went black. Everything was silent. She opened her eyes. She was in a room. There were seven doors. She walked over to one. Her hand touched the handle. She turned it. The door opened …

Alice Finney (12)
Trinity Catholic High School, Woodford Green

Short Story

I hadn't returned home in years. I hadn't wanted to leave my homeland, but in a way I had no choice. I looked over my city as a faint smile pulled on my lips. My black-midnight hair blew to the side under my dark red cloak's hood, it whispered in front of my deep brown eyes as I took in the sight that sat before me. I wore a long-sleeved red top with gold fastenings and threading, it came down to my thighs as my black trouser came from under it, tucked into my brown leather knee-high boots, and of course my red cloak, to show that I was an accomplished sorcerer. I looked upon the city and took in every detail from the sight, from the thatched roofs on the houses to the eerie glow of bonfires and lanterns. I sighed as my horse, Moonfire, sniffed my hand, her dark eyes weary from travelling like mine.

'C'mon Moonfire, time to seal our fate.' I stroked her neck and climbed onto the saddle. I pulled out a dark-coloured travelling cloak and wrapped it around myself to hide my red clock. Moonfire snorted in disapproval. 'Eh, Moonfire, I can't let anyone see me until we meet the king and queen you know that.' I comforted my horse and stroked her deep brown fur. I pulled up my hood to hide my face and swallowed, preparing myself for what lay ahead.

As we rode through the ankle-deep mud I cautiously looked at the people. Their faces sad and haunted. Moonfire and I attracted several looks of curiosity and suspicion. I urged her to go a little faster and then turned left.

'Back again are we?' smirked a figure in the dark alley. I grabbed for my bow and arrow, but it was too late as an arrow swept through the air and dug into my arm, Moonfire panicked in the commotion and threw me off, as I landed on the ground and blacked out.

Sarah Butt (13)
Trinity Catholic High School, Woodford Green

The Characters One Meets On A Train

One meets a great variety of characters on a train and with nothing else to occupy my attention, it becomes quite easy to detect their characters.

On one hand, is the solemn businessman dressed in a sombre suit, white shirt, starched collar and a bowler hat, carrying a black briefcase. He heads straight to the first class carriage, and sits, preferably alone. Next to a window where he can read his Financial Times without being disturbed. This is the last we see of him, the only reason we can tell he is still around is by the faint crackle of his newspaper.

On the other hand is the modern miss, returning from her shopping expedition in London. She struggles into the carriage, loaded with bags of various shapes and sizes, and stumbles a few times in her black stilettos before reaching her seat. She pulls out a compact mirror and some make-up and begins to powder her nose and reapply her coat of crimson lipstick. From this moment the journey is a continual rustle as she recalls her day's purchases.

Lastly, squashed into the corner balancing on the edge of the seat, is the very observer of this group, namely myself. Suddenly, with a screech of brakes, the train jerks to a halt and reaches my destination. I gather my luggage and amble to the door. With two pairs of eyes focused on me, it's now my turn to be observed.

Rosa Hurdidge (12)
Trinity Catholic High School, Woodford Green

Scary Story

It was a nice warm day, everyone was all happy and cheerful. It was a Monday, everyone was getting ready to go to school. Rosie and Jack were best friends, they would tell each other everything and do everything together. The school bell rang. Mr Brown was the form tutor of 8A, the form that Jack and Rosie were in. They had technology and English that day. It was their favourite because they liked practicals. When they're together their behaviour is bad, they distract other people and throw objects around the classroom.

'Rosie and Jack come here right now, why did you just throw that?'

'But Sir ...'

'Sir nothing! Detention for both of you. One hour after school.'

They arrived to the detention they had with Mr Brown. They had to sit there in silence all the time. Mr Brown told them to get the books that were in the other room, so they went to get them and when they returned Mr Brown was not there, they didn't know what to do, they were getting worried. Suddenly the lights went off, they started running, they went to the exits but the doors were locked. They heard noises and a big figure was coming towards them, getting closer and closer. The figure was holding something in his hand, as he was getting closer they started running, but there was no escape. They remembered Mr Brown telling them that a weird creature comes out at night for children.

Scream ...

Christian Giraldo (13)
Trinity Catholic High School, Woodford Green

My Story

'It's all gonna be OK babe!' Rachel emphasised while comforting her friend.

'No! That's where you're wrong, that's where you don't understand what's going on, and you say you do! I can't believe that you, my best mate can be so insensitive!' I argued. I can't believe how selfish she is being lately! She says that she understands and all that crap, but she doesn't! She's no naïve! 'And you wanna know the other thing that makes my blood boil?'

'No, but I'm pretty damn sure you're gonna tell me,' Rachel grunted.

'Yeah, you're right, I am gonna tell you. You tell me about how your life is so hard for you, you tell me that you are grounded and you expect me to feel sorry for you? Well you know what, I don't. Because your life is so sweet, you have the world at your feet, you have two parents that love you. What do I have? A dead father and an alcoholic mother, and you're the one complaining to me. When do you hear me complaining to you? Never. So, to be honest, I really can't be bothered with this friendship because it's always one way. Your way!'

So there you have it, I was having a crap time at home with a drunken mother and no father to turn to. That's how it happened. Funny isn't it. My dad dies and my mum decides that she will deal with it at the bottom of a wine bottle. Every wine bottle in the house. To be precise. And then I go to school, and have to listen to my so-called best mate's 'problems' so I was having a crap time at school as well. Isn't life sweet … ?

Amie Bailey (13)
Trinity Catholic High School, Woodford Green

Solja Vs Kaos

I was always getting in trouble. I was following in my brother's footsteps. The day they decided to release me from jail on bail, I swore never to get involved in any gun crime ever. Back on the estate I was known as Dirty Solja and lots of people knew this meant trouble. Word got around that I was back, this meant revenge from the yardie. The yardie hated the people who I hung around, and when they lost one of their members and heard I was involved, trouble struck.

The first thing that I did when I reached home was to catch up with my mate. My friend saved my life, but he let me go down for something I didn't do. Kaos was a no-good, dirty, lying, cunning person when it came to cops, he left you and claimed he'd never met you.

Kaos came up to me bowling it down the streets. 'Yo Solja, good thing you're back we have business to attend to,' he said with so much force, it made me tremble.

'Nah man, I not doing any of that no more, I'm a changed man,' I replied nervously.

'Changed man are you Solja? When you were about to get shot were you a changed man then, huh? Look, I hate to do this but if you don't help me, I'll bring your family into it and the first bullet will hit your mother.'

Thinking he was joking I refused, pulled up my trousers to my waist and left.

The next day rumours started flying that I was in beef with Kaos and you know what they say where there's smoke there's fire so I prepared to face him. It wasn't long before I had a shot at my house. When I got there I found my mum dead on the floor, in fear I took my brothers and left. I went and got myself a gun and decided to go after Kaos.

When I reached Kaos' house I fired shots and had some fire back. Realising I was OK I continued, that's when I saw blood and realised my brother, my one and only little brother, had been shot. I went back home carrying his body crying.

Wrote down my whole life, which didn't take long, and pointed the gun to my head and fired 'cause all I ever lived for was gone.

Patricia Wasonga (13)
Trinity Catholic High School, Woodford Green

Disaster Strikes

Drip, drip, drip, drip … That was the only noise I could hear. If it dripped one more time I could swear I would scream. There it went again. I got up out of my bed and walked into the bathroom. My feet touched the cold, tiled floor of the bathroom and I gasped from the chill. I clapped my hand over my mouth to stop me screaming. The bathroom window was open as my dad liked to keep the house freezing. I could smell the fresh morning air and also the dampness of the rain which had fallen the night before.

I tiptoed across the floor and reached the tap. I twisted the tap until it stopped dripping. I made my way back into my bedroom and sat on my bed. I reached over to my clock. It was 2.39am. I had around 2 hours left until my mum would be in to wake me up. I had to be at school at 7 as the coach was departing at 8 for the airport for the Year 8 ski trip.

A few hours later we were on the plane and all as hyper as each other: in a few hours' time we would be in Colorado. All of a sudden we were all jolted forward. The seat belt light was flashing and we were all ordered back to our seats. Bangs and crashes could be heard all around us. We were all being thrown around. The next thing we knew there was a man standing at the front of the plane dressed all in black, holding a gun. The man ordered us to sit down and be quiet otherwise we would all die!

Sophie Palmer (13)
Trinity Catholic High School, Woodford Green

Close Encounter

Late spring, 8am.

I am ready to go to school now, only needing to get on my bike to get to Monday's first lesson. I get on my bike steadying my balance, and pedal down the road. Once I reached the forest I started speeding up to 20mph. This place worries me, gives me the creeps. Then suddenly, in the corner of my eye, I see a light. I am getting really creeped out now. I meant, the forest was normal before ... then out of nowhere I heard a gunshot, and almost immediately my bike fell over and collapsed. I was hit in the head with one of the handles while tumbling, and winded myself. It turned pitch-black.

I don't remember anything after that except, that I could smell fire. I must have fallen unconscious. I woke up and looked around, 360 degrees. I was lost. I began to run. Any direction would do as long as I exited this eerie place. I heard gunshots again, and one went whizzing past my head. I had to run. Fast. Then dozens of bullets came my way. Oh no, I thought I'd die. I ran. Faster than before, determined to leave. I ran and ran; the place never seemed to stop. Avoiding trees and bushes, I shut my eyes with agony, using so much strength to sprint. I was worn out; slowed down and stopped. Breathing deeply, I opened my eyes and found myself out.

Dominic Cheah (13)
Trinity Catholic High School, Woodford Green

Scramble!

'Scramble!' someone shouted, the bell was ringing, everyone ran to their planes. The smell of burning petrol went everywhere, the Spitfires shot into the air, it was a glorious sight. The German bombers were everywhere, but they were no match for the Spitfires. Then the German fighters appeared, it was a fierce fight. Wherever you looked a fight was taking place.

However, the German fighters were no match for the Spitfires, but during the conflict one pilot was murdered. Lt John W Waters' plane was hit, he managed to open his cockpit but he couldn't get out, the burning petrol fumes were choking him, he had to get out, a fighter was on his tail, he still couldn't get out. He started praying to God then, as if by a miracle, he jumped out of the plane, he opened his parachute and was saved. He floated down and down, then a stray enemy fighter flew towards him.

When he landed all that they could find was his parachute riddled with bullets.

Joseph Clarke (13)
Trinity Catholic High School, Woodford Green

The Birthday Party

Everything was prepared for little Emma's 10th birthday party. The food was laid out on the table, there were sandwiches, cocktail sausages, sweets, ice cream, crisps and of course the cake. It was a yellow cake with daisies all over it. Though that was nothing compared to Emma's dress. It was pink with tiny rosebuds around the neck and along the hems. But she had forgotten the most important thing, how could she have a birthday party without a sacrifice?

But luckily for her one of her friends brought one. It was Julie Williams, a snobby little girl who had got them into trouble earlier that week. Her hands and feet were bound and her mouth was gagged. They bought her down to the basement. It was dark, dingy and riddled with damp. A perfect place for the sacrifice. They tied her down to the sacrificial table, it was in the shape of a pentagram. With candles made from congealed blood and paraffin at each of the points, Emma and her four friends donned matching black robes and stood at each point of the pentagram holding their hands over the flames.

Emma took the blade of the jackal and raised it above her head. Her friends were chanting ancient incantations that have been spoken at rituals such as these for over a millennia.

A look of pure unrestrained terror reached across Julie's face. She tried to get free but she was tied too tight, she watched as her life was about to end. Emma bought down the blade plunging it deep into Julie's heart. Julie's face was contorted with pain, as her body writhed and her crimson blood pulsed out of the wound. Her life force ebbing away. She died.

One week later, news report.

'Shock, Horror!

Horror struck the hearts of millions today as five little girls were convicted of murdering a fellow classmate. The victim was Julie Williams, they had brutally stabbed her to death in a demonic ritual of the occult. It has been reported that Julie Williams wasn't the first to be killed by these demented little girls. But that isn't the worst part, the questions on everybody's lips was how could this be going on in such a small town without anybody noticing? And what were the parents doing when this shocking crime against humanity was going on?'

Rosemary Acres (14)
Trinity Catholic High School, Woodford Green

The Travellers

Beep! Beep! Tiffany's alarm rang. As she pressed it she realised what day it was. It was her day to travel with her best friend, Amy. They had been planning it for ages. She finally managed to pull herself up from bed.

Tiffany is very lazy but very clever; her best friend, Amy, on the other hand is awake and raring to go.

Ding-dong the doorbell rang. 'Oh no!' she exclaimed. 'Amy's here.' She quickly rushed to get suitable clothes, for walking in, and then let her in.

'Hi Tiffany, are you ready?' Amy said excitedly.

'Yes,' Tiffany said, sounding tired.

So off they set on a long journey travelling through the mountains. It was very hot, as hot as the sun. Amy was a long way in front of Tiffany as she struggled to climb up the hill. She was doing the best that she could, but just could not take the scorching heat anymore. She sat down to savour a quenching drink. She shouted to Amy, 'Hold up, I'm just stopping for a drink.'

She was waiting for a response. There was no answer. She shouted again. 'I'm just stopping for a drink.' Still no response.

Tiffany was getting worried, so she hauled herself up from the ground and carried on walking to try and find Amy. As she was walking faster she could hear a loud cry.

'Hellll!'

Tiffany said to herself, 'That must be Amy, yes, it's Amy.' Tiffany saw that Amy had fallen down a ditch. She screamed, 'Hold on, I'm coming, don't worry ...'

Kathryn Baum (13)
Trinity Catholic High School, Woodford Green

The Jungle Warriors

In the depths of the Amazon Jungle there lived a large tribe of people called the 'Hydias' and Dunam, who was the leader of the tribe, is kind of like a king, protects and controlls the tribe. Unfortunately, in the capital city of Brazil, Brasilia, a group of archaeologists were searching for a lost relic worth trillions of pounds and they wanted to get their hands on it. However, the Hydias had looked after this historic and sacred relic for centuries and they weren't going to stop protecting it for a group of greedy men.

On the 14th July 1986, the Brazilian group found the whereabouts of the relic and started heading towards it, not knowing that Dunam was building up an army with spears and bows and arrows because his guide and his God, 'Hehdod', told him to make a small but aggressive and professional army. Hehdod did not tell him why he must do this duty but he did tell him to be prepared and aware of anything.

On the 29th July 1986, the Brazilian group entered the village but no one was to be seen, even so they felt happy and relieved that nobody was about to stop them. They entered the cave where the sacred relic was sitting on top of a stone where a beam of light was squeezing itself through a small crack in the roof of the cave onto the relic, which made it stand out in the cave.

The small Hydia army attacked from the cave and snatched the relic from the men's hands. They then took the men to the sacrifice area where the tribe hung the men and fed them to their animals, which weren't fed a lot anyway, so they were quite happy.

Adam Bishop
Trinity Catholic High School, Woodford Green

An Evening At The Nightclub

One Saturday night in the dead of winter we arrived as per our usual schedule, but the bar was filled with country hicks. I am not sure if there was a trailer park convention in town, but things just weren't right. This club was not always the 'in place', but I had never seen it look like that before. We looked around for a few minutes, got some drinks and went upstairs to play some pool. We were having a lot of fun kicking the kids' (well about 18-years-old!) butts in pool, but by about 11pm we were ready to hit the dance floor. We went to our usual spot on the front right of the stage, but there was a group of 'big hairs' dancing in a circle. We made our way to the middle of the circle and started dancing. These chicks were obviously perturbed that we were dancing in their territory, but the dance floor was packed and we had nowhere else to go.

They started trying to push us around by pretending that it was the music and that they had no control over their movement. Evelyn and I towered over them (over 6-feet in height) so we were laughing at them trying to push us. Finally after about 10 minutes of this pushing rubbish, we were getting fed up. I told one of the girls that if she pushed me again, I would make sure that she was kicked out of the bar (I was good friends with the manager - lucky!). Next thing I knew, out of nowhere, I felt a fist ... breaking my nose. I was so shocked that I just stood there with blood dripping all over my clothes. I don't think I have ever been so ticked off in my life.

Will Swistak (12)
Trinity Catholic High School, Woodford Green

Haunted House

She quickly shoved the key into the lock as a cold mist of winter met with her body. Reluctantly she entered as it was opened. It was late and all she wanted to do was fall fast asleep, so she sighed and slumped into bed and pulled the bedroom door shut.

A few hours later she was awoken by her bedroom door slowly creaking open, and the cold wind lurked in like a mysterious spirit. Reminding herself that she had closed windows and doors, she stumbled out of bed and firmly closed her door.

Creak, creak, a second time the creaking door awoke her and she rolled out of bed a second time to prove to herself nothing was there.

As she clutched the cold door handle she remembered she'd closed and locked all doors and windows, but as she opened the ever-creaking door she couldn't be more wrong, the door was wide open.

The wind and mist violently came rushing in and filled the room, the windows were also open and the flapping of the curtains broke the fearful silence. As she turned around to take in such a shocking image, her heart missed a beat as her door was covered in words smeared in blood. She took a deep breath and read the bloody words that terrified her a lot more than the *creak, creak*. The words 'Turn around' had dripped into each other, but she could read it clearly.

A rush of terror, fear and fright took over her, and what she feared most was taking two steps to face the other way, she dreaded turning around, she knew what was awaiting her.

Kasia Chinery (13)
Trinity Catholic High School, Woodford Green

Dear Boss ...

(A moment in the life of Jack the Ripper)

Daddy talks to me. Hidden yet among the voices. Voices that itch and twitch, voices that crawl and drawl, voices that shatter and scatter good thoughts and tell me to do dark things in darker places. Daddy talks to me, tells me that I am pure. He tells me of Mother. Whore, demon, evil Mother. He tells me of how he killed her, to purify himself, after he slept with her. Daddy the priest, who gave sleep to demons like me.

No! I force the memories back, swirling torrents of black ink inside my head, push them down and under, repressing Daddy's lessons. I wish he had not taught me so well. I hate him for being with my mother. Torrents of ink run down me. I am soaked to the soul. I am covered in ink, red ink.

I stand away from her body, drenched in her ink. Dried red ink. How long did I lie there? Listening to hidden voices? The woman sleeps so quietly, like one dead. So cold. So quiet. So demonic, she is a whore. I hate her. Hate her! I get my knife and cut her, over and over. Red ink hits me and splashes me and drenches me right to the soul. Still I hate her. Now, she is not dead, or asleep, she is nothing.

I dip a quill into her ink, her blood-red ink and begin to write.

Dear Boss ...

Owen Gardiner (14)
Trinity Catholic High School, Woodford Green

Haunted House

There it was that sudden creak, the noise shot through the air like a bullet out of a gun. The floorboards were ancient, dusty and broken in some places. Especially on the rickety stairs and now it sounded like someone was trying to creep up on them but doing a very bad job of it.

My heart was thumping in my chest, I could feel it pounding like a beater against a drum. It sounded ten times as loud as normal in the silence that spilt through the air.

I pulled my blanket over my head trying to shield myself from what was coming. An owl hooted at the window breaking the atmosphere, then I heard it again, the creak. Louder, coming quicker and closer.

I couldn't stand it any longer. I clenched my fists, my nails cutting into my hands, pain soaring through my skin. But I didn't care all of my focus was on the door. I swept over and pulled a shaking hand towards the handle of the door and turned it. I pulled it towards me, a tall, dark figure was standing there with a glass. I gritted my teeth, flung open the door and charged at the figure, not before I saw three small people (my sisters) hurtling out of their rooms.

The glass was lying on the floor, water trickled out as the glass lay smashed to pieces. I could hear a mixture of laughing and screaming, it was not a burglar after all, it was my dad, he had gone down to get a glass of water. Everyone was shrieking with laughter as he got up, even my mum was laughing. I don't think he'll go walking in the dark again in a hurry!

Katy Vinning (14)
Trinity Catholic High School, Woodford Green

Troubled Sleep!

It's 6.45 and Mother, the heart of the family, is lovingly preparing the family's evening meal.

'Ahh how can I tell Mark about Bethany's school report. It will tear him apart. Bethany has always been his favourite. It's going to break his heart. I can't keep it from him though!'

Just as the mother of the house is pondering what to do, Mark, her husband, falls through the front door, and slams it behind him.

'Evening darling? Good day?' Mark asks inquisitively.

'Yes honey! It was great, but ...'

'But what?'

'Ohh it's nothing really, forget it.'

'OK dear, if you're sure it's nothing, is dinner nearly ready?'

'Er yes, in about five minutes it will be.'

'Great I'm starving.'

While Mother is setting the table and Mark, her beloved husband, is reading the day's news from the local paper, the children are upstairs fighting over the computer, and as usual Bethany always loses to the two boys. Life's hard for Bethany against her two brothers, but she's always been Daddy's little girl, and Dad has always sided with her. Zak and Leo have always been jealous of Bethany for her being Daddy's favourite.

'Kids! Dinner's ready!'

A stampede to get to the dinner table would have been the usual way, but Bethany didn't want to fight with her brothers and she certainly didn't want to be in her parents' company when her dad found out about her little incident today at school. Conversation at the dinner table was always kept to a minimum. When dinner was finished the kids rushed away and Mother told Mark about Bethany's fight at school, and Mark flew off the handle. Mark and his loyal wife flew into a blazing row.

Mark put his shoes back on and flew out the front door and sped off in his flash Porsche.

'Here we go again, another argument. Why the hell am I always the black sheep of the family? Why did my stupid Mum have to tell Dad. Dad never had to know, she knows I'm the apple of his hazel-brown eyes!'

Dad didn't come back. Everyone was beginning to wonder where he had gone, but at about 10.30pm the phone rang, everyone bolted to the phone, but Leo got there first and answered the phone with a sharp, 'Yes?'

A police officer was at the other end. Leo panicked and dropped the phone. Mum had wonderful reflexes and caught the phone before it hit the ground. The police officer explained that Mark had been killed in an accident and when she got off the phone, Mother explained what had happened and that night Bethany couldn't get a wink of sleep. She blamed herself and as she thought she felt sick with guilt and sorrow that filled her clear blue eyes, and somehow seemed to darken the clear light blue to a dark murky colour. Everyone was going to blame Bethany. Bethany knew she had to do something … but what exactly? She just didn't know. *Everyone's going to blame me,* she thought! Death doesn't sound so bad, it sounds quite peaceful, maybe the sleeping tablets Mother takes might help me on my way …

Rebecca Mitchell (14)
Trinity Catholic High School, Woodford Green

Giving Up Is A Loss

I hated life, still do, I blame it on my young marriage. After all, if I hadn't have married him, I wouldn't have had a divorce. I wouldn't feel as sorry for myself as I do now.

Flicking through our memories, I strolled along the local beach. The sun beamed an orange ray. The sea glistened. An occasional breeze brushed through my hair, and I just watched and happily listened.

Soft, silky, sand found itself between my toes, whilst the salty sea crawled its way past my feet. This was the most enchanting day of my stressful week.

Irritatingly my phone rang, interrupting the silence. I failed to answer, ending up having to listen to the voicemail. It was my lawyer. Finally it was official, the divorce papers had gone through. I was now an independent woman battling the world alone. Was I really happy? Is this what I wanted?

Kicking away at the lifeless shells, I realised I had made a bad decision. I was now lifeless. Suddenly all the good memories of us together flocked like sheep. I remembered when I was crying and needed a shoulder to cry on and when I was cold, and he opened his arms to keep me warm. He was there. He was my first love; I was his. A few rows and arguments should not have resulted to this.

I had made up my mind, I would give him a call, maybe we could work things out.

Later, my phone rang. I did not hesitate to answer. Never to know this would affect my life. I began to speak with a radiant smile. The caller spoke.

'Hello, I am afraid I have terrible news - Michael is dead.'

I could remember dropping the phone as I fell to my knees. A tear passing down my cheek. I couldn't believe my love had died. I wanted to give our relationship just one more try.

Aderonké Boisson (14)
Trinity Catholic High School, Woodford Green

A Day In The Life Of Theo Walcott

Today, Monday 8th May 2006 I'm taking my driving theory test. I'm very nervous. Hopefully I'll do well. I need to concentrate.

I'm about to take the test and I'm really feeling the nerves. The test looks really long. It isn't too hard but it's going on for ages. I hope I've done well.

It has just finished, I'm going to get my phone and call my parents. 'Hello ... oh my God! You are joking. My dad's just told me that I am in the England World cup squad, he can't be serious? It can't be true. I've only played 23 games for Southampton and I haven't even played for Arsenal yet.

I'm just going to listen to the radio on my phone to see who has made the squad. 'Owen, Rooney, Walcott.' *What!* I don't understand, why me? This is great. First I moved to Arsenal and now this, it's unbelievable.

I need to ring Melanie, my girlfriend, to tell her the news. She won't have heard because she's still in school. We are going to celebrate, this is great.

Ring, ring my phone's ringing, it's Sven, the England boss, he has just told me I can come with the rest of the squad to Portugal for training if I want to. I can't believe this, my life just gets better every day. I can't wait. All of this and I'm only 17 years old! This is a dream come true for me. This is great!

Luke Fonseca (14)
Trinity Catholic High School, Woodford Green

She Returns ...

The sky was glowing a bright white from the moon. The thunder clashed and the sudden flash revealed an old gothic house. A small girl with black hair was standing there at the window waiting, barefoot. Her hair covered her face, she sucked her thumb, saying over and over, 'Mummy, where are you?'

She started to open the window. It was cold. A freezing draught blew through the house. The little girl shivered. She heard a thump. And then another. They were footsteps. Big ones. They grew even louder. She ran through the corridor after corridor, opening the doors and running through. She opened a smaller door. The footsteps stopped. She could hear him breathing long, deep breaths. She backed to the wall but fell. She could taste the mixture of sweat and blood.

The doors slowly opened.

Andrew Singer (14)
Trinity Catholic High School, Woodford Green

Introduction To The Chapters Of Laura The Great

Freedom, listen to the way the words ripples from your throat, dances on your tongue and licks your lips. 'Freedom' eight simple little letters which stood far from Laura Bank's door. Laura was an 82-year-old spinster and yet you never would have guessed that 60 years ago at the age of 22, Laura was known as 'Laura the Great'.

Each wrinkle she wore told a new story from the ones that told her dramatic childhood to 'Laura the Great' and all the way up to celebrating her 80th birthday. Laura was a woman with a life more unpredictable than the weather, she'd had her ups and her downs but nothing could keep Laura from living life to the full.

Laura had kept many secrets over the years other than her mind, the only other thing that contained these were a book of her life telling everything. Laura didn't need to read the book, she contained everything needed and she kept it so tightly locked up that her lips looked as though if she opened them the untold truth wouldn't stop pouring.

A year later she had become a prisoner of herself, she was locked in a world of her own, but just to remind herself of her past as 'Laura the Great' she'd written a book. Sadly that year Laura's book became the only thing that held her memory, and little did Laura know it would be shared to the world.

Rosie Wakefield (14)
Trinity Catholic High School, Woodford Green

The Bank Robbery - The Victim's Point Of View

Down on the floor, the cold marble floor, we are the hostages and they're in charge. Robbing the bank is a stupid thing to try, yet it still happens. My heart is pounding and the sweat is dripping down, I feel like a hippo in a sauna.

The robbers were walking towards the women and children with their air rifles, trying to scare them by shooting past them. That burns me up, but I can't do anything, but keep telling myself not to be a hero, not to be a hero. Time seemed to slow down, all I could see were mothers comforting their children and the rest of the hostages whimpering on the floor. I could still taste the blood in my mouth from when they hit me. I could smell the smoke from the gun.

They were getting bored so they went back to the mothers and their children bullying them into silence. They were urging the hero in me out, I was trying to hold it … it was too late. I didn't know what I was doing. It was happening too fast, I had suddenly got up and hit one of the robbers. That was my first and last mistake as a hostage. I suddenly felt a number of hot pieces of lead piercing through my flesh with the smell of gunpowder overwhelming me. It was all over, my life and time as a hostage.

Courtney Florent (14)
Trinity Catholic High School, Woodford Green